Geir Keys

Sounds of the Sixties

The Stories
Behind the Songs

First published in Great Britain in 2004 by OTK Books Ltd

Copyright © Geir Keys, 2004

Cover design and illustrations by Bernt Kristiansen

A CIP catalogue record for this book is available from the British Library.

ISBN 0-9548073-0-8

Printed and bound in Great Britain by
The Bath Press, Bath

Distribution by Central Books, 99 Wallis Rd., London E9 5LN
Tel: (0)20 8986 4854 e-mail: orders@centralbooks.com

OTK Books Ltd
One Friar Street
Reading RG1 1DA

e-mail: geirkeys@frisurf.no

Contents

Introduction 5

Eleanor Rigby 7
A Picture of You 17
Yellow Submarine 23
Those Were the Days 33
Death of A Clown 41
Lola 49
The Fool on the Hill 59
Viva Bobby Joe 65
Losing You 73
Norwegian Wood 81
Son of a Preacher Man 87
King of the Road 95
We Gotta Get Out of this Place 101
The Long and Winding Road 111
No Milk Today 121
Ferry Cross the Mersey 133
Ob-La-Di Ob-La-Da 141
Like I've Never Been Gone 151
The Carnival is Over 161
Penny Lane 167

Introduction

We all remember them, those wonderful songs of the Sixties, from a time of innocence and optimism when everything seemed possible for everyone, and many achieved the impossible dream that we all had, and lived it for the rest of us, who did not.

We remember the lyrics and the melodies, and the singers and musicians who introduced them to us. We remember the stories they told through their music. Some were very basic, while others again, were lyrical masterpieces that touched our emotions and conjured up pictures in our minds that were individual for each of us.

But they all told their tale within the framework of a few bars of music. Three verses and a chorus was all it took and all we got. Two to three minutes that left us asking for more, or perhaps, wondering why?

The composers of these songs were inspired by people or events that had consciously, or otherwise, made a greater or lesser impression on them at some stage of their lives.

The results were sometimes forgettable, but often remarkably memorable, and there has arguably never been produced more memorable music than that of the Sixties.

But when the music stopped, we were often left with a feeling of "What happened then?" or "Why did it happen at all?" After all, there is only so much you can say in three minutes, and remember, those three minutes also included a guitar break …

Why was Eleanor Rigby buried alone? Who was Lola? Why did they call it the Yellow Submarine? Who was the King of the Road? And what caused the Death of a Clown?

This book will try to tell you, by adding to the canvas on which the three verses of the original songs was painted, to give you the stories behind the songs you will always remember, from a time when we were all a little younger.

Sounds of the Sixties: The Stories Behind the Songs.
The first compilation album (Play at 33 rpm, and don't scratch the vinyl).
Geir Keys

"All the lonely people,
where do they all come from?"
Eleanor Rigby
(Lennon & McCartney)
The Beatles "Revolver" LP 1966

Eleanor Rigby

"Miss Rigby!"

The middle-aged woman gave a start as the deep voice broke through the silence of the empty church, startling her with its deep resonance as it echoed between the stone structures and implanted itself in her preoccupied mind.

She turned quickly, her heart beating, and saw the priest approaching her as he stepped down from the choir. "Yes, Father?" she managed in a plaintive voice that hardly carried back to him. She wore a grey woollen coat that was buttoned to her throat, and a small hat perched primly on the mousey brown hair of her head. She held her handbag against her stomach with both hands as if to protect herself, and watched with some apprehension as the priest came closer, nervously biting her bottom lip as he approached.

The priest smiled at her condescendingly. "Are you finished?" he asked.

"Yes, Father."

"The psalm books in place?"

"Yes Father."

"The flowers?"

"I've done them all, Father". Her voice tried to assure him that it was true. Her eyes implored him to believe her. She fidgeted with her fingers on the stitching of the handbag.

The priest nodded. "I'm sure you have Miss Rigby." He widened his smile as though to enfold her in his presence. "I know I can always rely on you."

She looked down at her feet, waiting. Her mind was blank. There was nothing there to occupy it, and there was an embarrassing silence that she was unable to fill, not knowing what to say.

The priest broke it. He had been looking expectantly at her face, as though willing her to say something, but finally broke the trance with a sigh. "Then I'll see you later, at Evensong." This was a statement rather than a question, but neither of them noticed the fact. She had always done what was expected of her, naturally following her instinct to do what others told her rather than making her own decisions, and the priest had come to expect nothing less of her.

She raised her eyes slowly, but without allowing them to reach his face, and whispered "Yes, Father", before he walked away from her.

Eleanor Rigby had always felt insecure. Her extreme shyness made it impossible for her to establish any kind of relationship with others. She had had no friends when she was a child. At school she had been alternately ignored or teased by the other children, and often tormented by the teachers who saw her vulnerability and abused it, perhaps in an attempt to enhance their stature in their own eyes, and in those of the children they were responsible for.

She lived alone with her widowed mother in a small, brick house in an endless row of similar houses. One of the thousands that lined the streets of the city, the bricks that had once been red and new, now old and black. A poor home with few comforts, yet the only haven she had from the misery she experienced once outside it. She was the first and only child her mother had, as she had almost died in childbirth at the age of fortythree, and there had been no thought of tempting fate by bringing another child into the world. Her father had been killed in a mining accident when she was still a child. She could hardly remember him, but nonetheless treasured the old black and white photograph that stood in its frame on the mantelpiece above the fireplace in the small living room where they spent their time alone, with little to discuss, and even less to entertain them. Time passed with the help of books from the library and the BBC on the radio.

Although her memories of her father were few, she dutifully found her way to his grave twice every week. Always on Tuesday and Saturday, and always just before dusk. She would have a small gardening spoon in her bag, and a few small flowers held in her hand, and she would talk to her father as she turned the soil and placed the flowers in it. Here she could talk openly about her thoughts and her feelings, and about the uneventful pitifully anonymous life she led, as it passed her by day by day. Here she felt at peace, knowing as she did, that her father heard her, and understood.

She never found employment, although she tried. A few minutes in none-receptive silence with her, was enough to convince any prospective employer that she would be unsuitable for whatever the work entailed. Her days were therefore as lonely as her nights, with no-one to communicate with, or to share her life with.

The only sanctuary she ever found was in the church. There she could be among other people sharing a common activity, and feeling a part of them, while still remaining anonymous amongst them. She became a regular visitor, and never missed a service, but always placed herself in a pew that was far to the back and to the side, and as far from others as possible.

She would sing with the others during the services, but no-one else would ever hear her voice, for she sang quietly, afraid that others might hear her. But she heard her own voice, a voice that few ever heard, and in her mind she could hear herself singing the words of praise loudly and clearly, and it made her happy for the few moments the hymn lasted. When the service was over she would be the first to leave, never having exchanged a word with anyone, and walking quickly back to her home, to spend the rest of the day with her mother.

Thus, Eleanor Rigby's life passed slowly and uneventfully, evolving as it did, between the church, her father's grave, and her mother's home. She was never happy, but she was content, having accepted her fate, and knowing no other life to compare it with.

She was thirtyfive when her mother died. The old lady had been ill for some time and had been bedridden for the last two years of her life. As her own boredom and fear of death increased, her demands on her daughter became greater. Eleanor Rigby nursed her mother through her illness, and only left her when she went to church. The old lady would rant against her hours before she was to leave, accusing her of mistreating her and not caring if she lived or died, and Eleanor Rigby would often find herself in tears as she closed the door on the terraced house behind her, and moved in the direction of the church, always feeling the weight of her guilty conscience heavy upon her shoulders. Sometimes, she was quite unable to leave, feeling too shattered by the accusations thrown at her by her mother, and she would instead remain with her, in lonely and abject misery.

From this period, she could later only remember the sound of the walking stick being knocked repeatedly against the floor of the bedroom above, and the voice calling "Eleanor! Eleanor! I know you can hear me! Come up here at once!" And she would climb the stairs once again, feeling dejected, abandoned, lonely, and very, very tired.

When her mother finally died, Eleanor Rigby felt an intense guilt at the feeling of relief she experienced, and quickly smothered it, hiding it behind the overpowering loneliness she gradually felt overcoming her. Now nobody needed her. No-one knew her. There was nothing left of her childhood, her youth, or her life, because there was no longer anyone who had been a part of them. She was now completely alone, whereas there before had at least been someone to share her loneliness with her. Now there was no-one.

She now had two graves to care for, but never visited them on the same day although they both lay in the same graveyard. She continued to visit her father each Tuesday and Saturday, but now also went back each Monday and Friday to care for her mother's grave. By doing so, she helped to fill her week, having something to look forward to do four of the week's days rather than just two, as before.

She still talked to the father she could not remember, but found it difficult to open herself to the mother she had known all her life and who had shared her loneliness throughout it. It was somehow too personal to share her innermost feelings with someone who knew her too well. She therefore contented herself with greeting her mother with a quiet "Hello, Mum" when she came to her grave, and a "Bye, Mum," when she left it, sometimes adding a whispered "I miss you," as though to reassure her of her love. But every time she left her mother's grave, she found an uneasy feeling of guilt creeping over her, that she never felt when she left her father.

She had enough time to ponder upon this, and did so often, although without ever allowing herself to understand whatever reasons lay behind it. She insisted that she loved both her parents with equal affection, and often repeated this in her own mind, although sometimes doubting her own conviction. The doubt and conviction often emerged simultaniously to fight for her attention, and she would sometimes have to go between them to make them stop, and she would then try to focus on something else to get them out of her mind.

But there was so much time, and so little to fill it with. Although she pretended to live a busy life, she knew that this was a lie created to camouflage the truth, but she preferred to live the lie rather than to face the truth of her own miserable existence.

It was Father McKenzie who suggested that she might want to help in the church. As luck would have it, he came upon her one day as she was leaving the church. They met in the doorway, and he happened to stand in her way, thus blocking the passage for the retreat she sought.

"Miss Rigby," he said, holding out his hand to shake hers. "How nice to see you." He lifted one reluctant hand from her handbag and shook it. It was the first physical contact she had had with anyone since her mother had died two years earlier, and she trembled at his touch.

"I've been wanting to talk to you, Miss Rigby," he continued, and lowered her hand back to the handbag. "You see, I'm quite hopeless at looking after the practical things that need to be done here in the church," he smiled self-depreciatively, "and I was wondering if you might consider helping me?" He saw the fright in her face, and quickly added, "It would only be for a few hours during the week – whenever it would be suitable for you – whenever you have the time …"

That had been many years ago. Since then Eleanor Rigby had had the time, and had found it suitable, to spend several hours of each day in the church, quietly doing the various tasks that needed to be done. Her life had changed in that she now had a responsibility to fulfill, and felt that someone needed her and was therefore aware of her existence, and the days now passed more quickly than they had ever done before.

She still kept entirely to herself, afraid to face other people and quite simply unable to communicate with them, but her life now had a meaning. She would wipe the dust off the pews, and wash the stone floor; she would replace the candles that had burned low in their holders, and arrange the numbers of the psalms and hymns in the displays; she would collect the hymnbooks and replace them in the bookcases after each service when everyone had left; she would do any menial task that was asked of her, and do so without question, only happy to know that she was needed.

And she was always in attendance at funerals that were held in the church, first making sure that the flower arrangements were in order, then distributing the hymnbooks to the mourners, before finding a place by herself from which she could sadly follow the ceremony. Although she had never had contact with any of the deceased or their families, she always shared their sorrow, somehow feeling a personal relationship existing between them; the deceased had lost his life, whereas she herself had never had one to lose.

The members of the church congregation were used to her, and had long since stopped trying to get through her shell of shyness, and now merely nodded in her general direction whenever they passed her in the church, and no longer reacted to the way she turned her head away from whoever seemed about to catch her attention.

The years passed by slowly, and in her own way, Eleanor Rigby was happy. She divided her time between her tasks at the church, participating at church services, visiting her parents, and the silence of her home. Throughout her life she had never once complained about the loneliness that had imprisoned her from the day she was born, but had eventually accepted it as being her lot in life. As long as she had the church, and Father McKenzie allowed her to help him there, she would be content in the knowledge that at least someone cared about her and realised her worth. And so her life passed uneventfully year after year, with neither warmth or comfort once entering it.

It was cloudy as she closed the door behind her and began to walk along the pavement towards the church, so she held a rolled umbrella in one hand, in case of rain. She had been feeling unwell for a few days, and blamed the change of weather from the warmth of late Summer to the colder evenings of Autumn.

She felt a spasm of pain in her chest as she approached the church, and she winced, but it quickly passed. She moved to a pew at the back of the church and bent her head to offer a prayer. As she was silently mouthing the words, she noticed that she was getting a headache, so she raised herself into an upright position and kneaded her brow with the fingers of her right hand as she concentrated on the service.

Halfway through it, she began to feel sweat come to her brow and a nauseous feeling gnawing at her stomach and her throat. She thought of getting up and going outside to get some fresh air, but was afraid to bring attention to herself, so she remained instead in her seat as she wiped her brow with her handkerchief and tried to take slow, deep breaths to overcome the nausea.

She fainted in the middle of the seventh hymn, and crumbled with a crash against the stone tiles, the disturbance causing the congregation to turn in her direction while the words of the hymn died on their lips as they saw her lying there.

They were soon by her side wanting to help. Father McKenzie pulled himself through the people surrounding her, and lowered himself towards her. He lifted her head to rest against his knee, patted her on the cheek to waken her, and called "Miss Rigby! Miss Rigby! Are you allright?" At the sound of his voice, she opened her eyes slowly. She tried to turn her head towards him, but it didn't move. A frail voice whispered "Yes, Father ..." So inaudibly that nobody heard it, then the eyes glazed over and her head rolled to one side against Father McKenzie, and Eleanor Rigby died, as quietly as she had lived.

Nobody knew her, so nobody came. Those who knew of her, hoped that others would attend the funeral, but these others obviously had the same hope, and therefore none came.

Nobody arranged the few flowers in the church that day, and Father McKenzie had to place new candles in the holders himself, for Eleanor Rigby was no longer there to do it for him. She lay in the casket at the foot of the steps leading up to the choir, where Father McKenzie stood and held a brief eulogy over her remains, finishing quickly as he looked into the empty church, for the first time in his life feeling completely inadequate.

Eleanor Rigby was buried alone with only Father McKenzie and two gravediggers in attendance. "From dust to dust and ashes to ashes", he said quietly, as he poured the grains of soil over the casket and thought of the sad and meaningless life she had lived.

Nobody remembered her. Nobody recalled what she had looked like or of ever having met or known her. Only Father McKenzie, and he was now an old man with little time left in this life. Sometimes Eleanor Rigby would enter his thoughts, and he would shake his head and allow a sad smile to linger on his lips. Then something would catch his attention, and she was gone again, as quickly as she had come. Forgotten in death as she had been in life.

Her grave lies in the far corner of the cemetery where few people ever go, some distance from her parents. The inscription on the stone is already beginning to fade, but can still be read:

E. Rigby
1901–1963
RIP

The grass around the stone is overgrown. There are no flowers. Eleanor Rigby lived, and died. But nobody noticed.

Do you Remember, Do you Recall 1960

- Harold Macmillan was Prime Minister.
- D.H. Lawrence's controversial Lady Chatterley's Lover was cleared of being pornographic in an Old Bailey verdict and could then be sold legally – gasp, gasp!!
- John F. Kennedy won the presidential election in USA beating Nixon by very few votes. (Vicious tongues claimed that Daddy called in old favours from his Mafia friends to fix the vote.)
- Gregory Peck and Ava Gardner were On the Beach.
- Peter Sellers fought Ian Carmichael for the trade union in I'm Allright Jack.
- Sandra Dee was in A Summer Place. (But where was Bobby Darin?)

Some popular records of the year that went right to the top:
- My Old Man's A Dustman: Lonnie Donegan making people happy
- Cathy's Clown: The Everly Brothers (Phil & Don to you)
- Three Steps to Heaven: A posthumous nr. 1 for Eddie Cochran who was killed in a car-crash during his tour of Britain. Old Rocker Gene Vincent survived the crash but was left with serious back injuries that jeopardized his career (pain-killers and booze are not a healthy combination).
- Apache: The Shadows proved they could do it without Cliff. Remember the original line-up? Try Hank B. Marvin (the guy with the glasses), Bruce Welch, Tony Meehan and Jet Harris.
- Only the Lonely: Roy Orbison – The Big O himself – starting a career that should have lasted forever with a voice that others could only dream of (In Dreams?).

*"I didn`t know your name what could I
do, I only had a picture of you …."*
A Picture of You (Beveridge/Oakman)
Joe Brown & The Bruvvers 1962

A Picture of You

"She'll be coming round the mountain when she comes, she'll be coming round the mountain, coming round the mountain …" They held the note as long as they could, some warbling their voices for show, then finished with gusto *"Coming down the mountain when she comes."* They cheered and applauded their own performance as the laughter and comments came thick through the cigarette smoke in the coach.

They were on the firm's annual day trip to Blackpool. Two coaches every year in early June full of fun and expectation, lewd jokes and high spirits, of both sorts. It had always been Blackpool, but nobody seemed to mind; after all there was plenty of whatever you wanted there, and people were used to the day trippers and their excesses. And why not? They brought their cash with them and knew how to spend it.

So it had also been Blackpool this year, from where they were now returning late at night, their money spent on pleasure, full of experiences that would become the memories of reminiscence as they later recalled the trip. But now they were just happy and tired and content to be on the way back home, with Blackpool just a blur of impressions waiting to clear with the light of the coming day.

As always at that time of the year the place had been packed with trippers up for the day with only one thing on their minds; to enjoy themselves in every way, as they milled along the streets and pressed into the pubs and cafes.

The coaches were parked in roads and streets and coach parks. Any where they could find a space. As each new coach stopped to open its doors, the passengers spilled out with expectancy on their faces and excitement in the loud voices that called about them.

But now they were on the way back, and the songs became fewer as the exertions of the long day mingled with the darkness of the night outside and the purring of the engine inside to lull them into uneasy sleep as the coach moved through the darkness of the night bringing them closer to home with each hour that passed.

Harry Warden rested his head sideways against the seat and stared into the night without seeing anything but the emptiness that passed by him outside. He was tired but he couldn't sleep. He was closing on fifty far too quickly for comfort, and dreaded the day as some kind of turning point in his life when things would only start going downhill, and he knew that you went faster down a hill than up it, so from fifty on he knew that the rest of his life would run away from him. "That was your life, that was," he thought. "Not much was it?"

He was a lathe operator on the floor of the factory where he had worked all his life. He enjoyed his work and considered many of his colleagues as friends, so he usually looked forward to each new day. He had been a widower for eight years after his wife was killed in a car accident, and he had then moved in with his sister to share her home. She was a spinster and liked to have a man around the house, while he had someone to cook his meals for him and wash his clothes. It was an amicable arrangement that worked well, although coming home was no longer what it once had been.

There had been no romance in his life since his wife had died. No woman had entered it, although he had sometimes thought of inviting one of the women from the factory out, but those few who were single were much younger than him, and he was afraid of making a fool of himself. He was part of the environment in his local pub where he had friends and acquaintances of both sexes, among whom he was well liked, but in the same environment there were no available women who interested him.

However he had become accustomed to his new life and accepted it, taking pleasure in the positive side of it while ignoring whatever pieces were missing, as though by doing so, they did not exist.

He lowered his eyes to his suit jacket and noticed that it had become crumpled during the course of the day. He remembered ironing it the day before to make sure he would look his best for the trip. It was his only suit and he rarely used it. The last time had been the previous year when they had made the same trip to Blackpool.

His eyes were staring inwardly at something that he could see in his mind. He blinked, then eased his wallet from his pocket, and slowly pulled out a photograph. He had taken it the previous year with a Brownie camera he had had with him. It was black and white. He looked closer and let the dim light from the corridor show the laughing face of a woman with a cowboy hat on her head and "Kiss Me Quick" lettered across it. She was holding a handbag in one hand while the other held the hat in place.

He smiled to himself as he thought of her excited chatter as she had climbed out of the helter skelter van at the fairground, smiling and laughing uncontrollably while he pointed the camera and pressed the shutter. She had come straight to him, taken him by the arm, and marched him unprotesting and happy, towards the spinning wheel. "This is fun, Harry!" she had whooped at him, "I'm having a great time!!" And he had put his arm around her as they went through the crowd.

They had met as total strangers but had somehow been thrown together, and found themselves enjoying each others company so naturally that they had stayed together for the rest of the day, only occasionally bumping into their respective friends as they bustled backwards and forwards with the crowds.

They did it all – wading in the sea, the donkeys, the various temptations of the fairground whether they went up and down or round and round, the sideshows … Everything! They had ended up in a dinner-dancehall late in the evening where they had danced to the music of the band.

It had been a fantastic day. He couldn't remember ever having enjoyed himself so much, or hearing so much laughter, most of which seemed to come from him. She had such an outgoing personality, so alive and exciting, and with so much infectious and effervescent energy, that she somehow raised him to her own level, and he felt alive like he had never felt before, like an excited child being drawn into a wonderland of lights and music and laughter.

Time passed so quickly. Too quickly! They had had to run to catch her coach, and arrived laughing and breathless just as it was about to pull away. He managed to give her a quick kiss as she stood on the steps with the doors open. He watched as the coach pulled away from the pavement then realised that he had not asked her name and shouted to her. She called back to him but he couldn't hear her above the sound of the engine accelerating, but only saw her lean out and wave to him. Then her head disappeared inside as the coach moved away into the night, and she was gone.

He had spent the next days in confusion and frustration, angry at himself for not having the intelligence to get her name and address, but time had passed so quickly and been too full to think that it would ever end, and it had simply not occurred to him to ask her.

He thought about her all the time. Couldn't get her out of his mind. One week later he had had the film printed, and the sight of her laughing face vividly brought her back to him, and for a moment they were together again at the fairground in Blackpool.

He had tried to find out who she was, or where she might have come from, but to no avail. He knew too little, and there had been far too many coaches and visitors to choose from. She was lost and he couldn't find her. He only had his memories of her, and of the fantastic day they had spent together. And her picture. That was all.

Although he had known that it was an impossibility, he couldn't keep hope off the coach that had now carried him back to Blackpool a year later, and he had restlessly wandered through the crowds throughout the day looking for her, wishing her to be there and hoping to see her face. Sometimes his heart skipped as he thought he saw her, but then his shoulders would sag back in place as he realised his mistake, and he would wander on despondently looking into every face he saw, although realising that he would never see hers again.

A voice broke the silence in the coach. "Right, everybody," a man called from the back, "Let's have a sing-song!" then began singing at the top of his voice, *"She'll be coming round the mountain when she comes, she'll be coming round the mountain when she comes."* A few tired voices joined in. *"She'll be coming round the mountain, coming round the mountain …"*

Harry Warden took a last long look at the worn picture in his hand, then carefully replaced it in his wallet. He stared at the roof of the coach then opened his mouth, and sang,

"... *Coming round the mountain when she comes ...* "

A letter arrived a week later. He did not recognise the handwriting on the envelope, and opened it, wondering what was inside. He unfolded the paper and began to read:

"Dear Harry,

I don't know if you remember me, but one of my friends who was with me on the trip last year happened to bump into one of your workmates in Blackpool last week, and ..."

*"In the time when
I was born, lived a
man who sailed to
sea ..."*

Yellow Submarine
(Lennon &
McCartney)
The Beatles
"Revolver"
LP 1966

The Yellow Submarine

The four men shared a table in the corner of the pub. It was seven o'clock in the evening. Although busy, it was still too early to be full, and the barman had time to enjoy a chat with one of the customers while he cleaned the glasses.

They were in their thirties, old friends who had known each other from childhood, sharing the boredom of schooldays, the excitement of their rebellious teens, and the commitments of marriage and mortgages, through all of which their friendship had survived.

Their voices joined with the others in the room to make a background of sound that enabled each customer the pleasure of talking aloud without having to be conscious of others overhearing what they had to say. The four men were conversing with no particular aims to their conversation but to enjoy it, and their words were often punctuated with laughter as they spoke.

Then one of the four lifted his eyes to look over the heads of the others, and broke into whatever was being said with a mild oath, "Oh god, don't look now, but he's here again!" He nodded towards the door. They all turned their heads to look. "Bloody Submarine Jack, himself!" he said with a sigh.

They followed the man with their eyes as he entered the room. "Captain Nemo, you mean," one of the others said.

"Who?" the third asked, turning towards him.

"You know. Captain Nemo." He saw no response in his friend's face. "20.000 Leagues Under the Sea? The sub?" He rolled his eyes in exasperation, and added, "Kirk Douglas in that old film?" He stared expectantly into the blank face before him, but got no reaction, so gave up. "Oh, forget it!" he said, and lifted the glass to his mouth as his eyes turned back to the man who had just entered the room.

He was older than them. Somewhere in his fifties. A small man in a crumpled black donkey jacket. He had a dirty white scarf around his neck and a collarless shirt was buttoned up to the throat as though to keep the chill off it. He wore heavy, worn boots studded with metal on the soles, that clicked against the wooden floor with each step he took. The cap on his head was well pulled down against the wind outside, yet at a cocky angle that seemed to have a message that could not be misunderstood. The jaunty swagger of his walk gave the same message, "Don't mess with me," it seemed to say. He went to the bar and bought a pint of mild beer, black as coal, and took a sip from it as he turned and casually viewed the room and its inhabitants.

The four men in the corner knew him, as everybody did. They had known him all their lives, and had been in awe of him since childhood when they had first heard the stories. Then, he had been a kind of hero to them, having heard of his exploits during the war. They had often asked him if they were true. He would confirm this, then give himself good time to elaborate the details of his life killing Germans and sinking their ships. Although the details sometimes changed from one telling to the next, he had always told the stories with animated intensity that had left them immensely impressed, with their minds conjuring up pictures of all he had told them. He was their hero. A war hero, and they had felt proud to know him.

Not now though. Not now when they were grown men. Not now when he had become a legendary trouble maker, brawling or drunk, and always in some kind of trouble. Just one step ahead of the police, with a conviction of some kind just waiting for him. They could still stomach all of this. After all, Liverpool in the early sixties was a place where you had to be able to look after yourself, and there were any number of tough men to avoid. He was just one of many.

What they couldn't accept was that they now found him boring. Whenever he found them with no means of immediate escape, he would always bring the rather stinted conversation back to the war and his role in it. They had of course, heard it countless times before. Whereas these stories had enthralled them as children, they now only despised the man for repeating them, even doubting their truth. The fact that the man they had once looked up to as their hero, had become a rather shabby figure, in dirty clothes, unemployed and unemployable, and with criminal tendencies, yet still cocking his head at the world as though he owned it, embarrassed them.

They had become quiet under the man's scrutiny, afraid that he would notice them and come to join them, and they kept their eyes to the table while they attentively nursed their glasses. "Oh, no …" one said quietly through his teeth, as he saw him approaching them through the corner of his eye.

"Evening gents," he saluted them jovially, "Mind if I join you?" he asked as he pulled up a chair and sat down, smiling at them.

They all moved around to give him more space as they smiled uncertainly and answered in chorus, "Of course," unnecessarily adding "sit down." Their nervousness made them overreact and they became animated in their attempts to open a conversation.

Their nervousness did not come from fear of the man or of his dubious reputation, but from the awkwardness they felt in his presence, each knowing that they had come to despise him for the man he had become. And for the feeling of betrayal they all felt after having wasted their childhood years in proud admiration of the man and his exploits, knowing them now to have been false boasts from a false man.

"Anyway, how are you Jack?" one of them asked in a strained attempt to keep the stinted conversation going on an open and friendly level.

Jack lowered the glass from his lips and replied with a non-commital "Not so bad", then placed the glass on the table, as he added, "I met one of my old shipmates yesterday." He glanced around the table and saw the four faces looking at him in silence, as they tried to hide their quiet despair, knowing what was coming. "I was with him on the subs," he explained, as if they didn't know. "Oh, God, here we go …." they thought in mute harmony.

"We were both on the yellow submarine", he went on. They were all brought back from their own thoughts when he caught them off guard, unexpectedly throwing out a question, "Do you know why we called it the yellow submarine?" he asked, and looked from one to the other.

They glanced around the table, and shrugged, "Because it was yellow …?" one tried. Jack laughed good-naturedly, "Not exactly," he said, "but it could have been." He finished lighting a Woodbine, "It could have been any bloody colour all the time we spent in the deep. Even polka-dot or stripes, and nobody would have known the difference."

He looked from one to the other, waiting for other suggestions. When none came, he offered the answer. "We spent weeks at a time inside that sub. Sometimes we'd be busy chasing the Krauts, and other times we'd be laying low hiding from the buggers while they tried to locate us. They knew we were there, and they hit us with everything they had of depth charges, while all we could do was to lie still under the water. We couldn't make a bloody sound or they'd hear it and locate our position."

His eyes were now staring at the table, and he was obviously back in the submarine again. He gave a short laugh, "We couldn't even fart, or they'd have pinpointed us, and that would have been that!" He looked up at them to make sure they understood. "Those charges were going off all around us, knocking us about inside. We were falling all over the bloody place, and just waiting for one to have a direct hit, and that would have been the end of us." He paused and took a long pull on his cigarette before continuing. "We were stuck like that for seven long hours, but it seemed like seven long years, and we all knew we were going to drown."

He fondled his glass between his hands and stared into it in silence, then brought it to his lips, took a swig and smiled, "But we didn't, did we?"

The four men looked at each other as though to say "…And, so what?" Instead, two of them asked in stereo, "So what's that got to do with why you called it the yellow submarine?"

The ex-submariner, smiled back at them. "We all pissed our pants, didn't we?" and laughed aloud.

"The whole bloody crew, officers and all. We all pissed our pants," and he laughed again. "That's when it became the yellow submarine, when we all pissed our pants with the bombs going off all around us, and we knew we were going to die."

He took a pause when his laughing had subsided, then pointed slowly from one to the other, and assured them "You would have done the same thing.

And you wouldn't even have noticed doing it." Then he leaned back in his stool and added "You'd better believe it," as he raised the glass for a new mouthful, which emptied it.

After a few minutes of strained small talk, with no offer forthcoming for a new drink, he got up. "Got to go," he said, "See you around," then left, moving through a group of new arrivals coming through the door.

"Thank God, he's gone," one of the friends said as he watched him go through the door. "I thought we were going to be stuck with him all night."

They discussed him for a few minutes, relaxed and relieved that he was gone, and they laughed as they imitated him. "I wonder what they would have called that bloody sub if they had shit their pants instead?" one asked, and they laughed again.

"Excuse me."

They turned to the voice. A well-dressed elderly man stood by their table with a gin and tonic in his hand. They recognised him as one of the group that had entered when the other man had left.

"Excuse me for butting in, but did you happen to know the man who just left a few minutes ago, the barman says he was with you?"

"Now what?" they thought, and answered suspiciously "Yes …?"

"Do you know his name? Could that have been Jack Shannon?"

They confirmed that was his name, while wondering what this was all about.

The elderly man cast a long look at the door, "Yes, I thought it was," he said thoughtfully. He sipped his drink without taking his eyes off the door, "I thought I recognised him." He turned back to the four faces who were looking questions at him. "But he really has changed quite a lot, hasn't he," he said quietly to himself. It was not a question, just an acknowledgement of fact.

A thought struck him. "Look, do you mind if I sit down for a moment?" They looked at each other as though to say "Why not?" then pulled the stool to one side for him to sit. He took a deep breath then asked "Did you know that he was in the navy during the war?" They mumbled affirmatives while they eyed each other and thought "Oh no, not again …"

Their new acqaintance turned towards the bar and called to the barman, "Could we have something to drink over here, please?" then turned back to them. "He was on the submarines throughout the war," he told them. "Five years underwater in those damned buckets." He shook his head as though in amazement, then looked up at them, "Not many people lasted that long you know."

The drinks came. After saluting him with their glasses, the buyer continued. "The submarines he served on were all involved in several incidents." The friends looked at each other at the use of the word "incident", then listened as their benefactor continued. "He was shipwrecked three times you know, and it's simply a miracle that he survived. All reports confirmed that he had behaved in an exemplary fashion each time. All in the best tradition of the navy." At this he raised his glass in salute, and they all followed suit feeling obliged to do so, and appreciating the opportunity to sip their beer.

"You may be wondering how I know all this," he said, then informed them "You see I was the commander of the squadron of submarines that he belonged to, so it was my job to know what was happening."

They all mouthed "I see's ...." While wondering where all this was taking them.

"Do you know what Jack is doing now?" he suddenly asked them. "How is he?"

They were surprised at the question, and sat up in their stools as they wondered how to reply. "Well, he's been out of work as long as I've known him," one said, and another added "He's got a tendency to get into trouble, brawls and stuff ..." he ended tamely, regretting he had said it.

The older man smiled sadly and looked down at his glass. "Yes," he said slowly, "That is often the case. What a shame. What a damned shame..."

They didn't break into his thoughts as he sat in silence, obviously reminiscing about something. After a few moments he stirred his drink and looked back at them. Their faces now held an inquisitive expectancy, as though waiting for some new revelation, the earlier boredom no longer showing.

"Five years is a long time, you know," he said. "A damned sight longer when you spend it in a sub in the depths." He thought for a moment, then said almost to himself "It's so bloody quiet down there. Like a tomb. If the depth charges don't get you, the silence will." He had their attention, and they held unto his every word.

"Jack was down there for five years, you know," he repeated, as though he had forgotten that he had already mentioned the fact. "That's a lifetime for a submariner. But he did get a few medals on the way." He gave a grunt, "Although I don't suppose they are worth much to anybody today." He looked up at them, "I mean, who cares anymore? The war has been over for years, so who cares?"

They didn't know how to react to this, so they said nothing.

"I believe I told you that Jack was shipwrecked three times?" He looked at them as they nodded their heads in unison. He registered their confirmation, then continued. "The third time was the worst for him. It happened in the north Atlantic in May of '44. They got caught, and stayed down for several hours while they were blasted by everything the Germans had. While the Krauts hoped that one of their bombs would hit their target, the poor buggers in the sub were praying that they wouldn't, and only chance and the Allmighty could decide who would win.

They knew they would be dead if a bomb hit them. They would either go to the bottom to drown, or be machine-gunned by the Germans if they were lucky enough to survive and reach the surface." He looked at them, "You know that they showed no mercy to the crews on our subs, don't you?" They didn't, but stayed quiet.

"As it happened, it was night when they were hit. The explosion tore a hole in the side and the water poured in, making it impossible to manoeuvre. They were in a death trap, and knew they were going to die, but they tried to save themselves in the only way open to them, and twelve of the crew managed to get out and reach the surface. Jack was one of them. The rest went to the bottom with the sub."

He took a pipe from his pocket and filled it, then put it to his mouth and lit it with a match. "The Germans couldn't see them in the darkness, and they had drifted far away from them by the time daylight came. Otherwise they would have shot them. Every man." He puffed on his pipe. "Try to imagine yourselves, gentlemen, shipwrecked in the middle of the Atlantic in only the clothes on your back and a lifejacket."

He stared into each face. "The Atlantic is a bloody big place, believe me." He decided to let his pipe rest, and placed it on the ashtray. "There were twelve survivors from the sub, but their chances of rescue were non-existent. They were going to die, and every man there knew it."

The four friends were now hanging on his every word, waiting for him to continue.

"God alone knows how it happened. It was a one in a billion chance, but after two days and nights in the water one of our ships stumbled upon them. Believe me, it was no less than a miracle. They pulled them out of the water one by one. Jack was the last of them. They found him holding one of the others, keeping his head over the water, as he incoherently babbled on encouragements to the man, "Keep going! We'll make it, mate, don't give in! We'll soon see old Blighty again!" on and on."

He took a deep breath, and shook his head. "He made the crew in the lifeboat take the other man on board first, calling to him as they did so, "There you are Charlie, I told you we'd make it!" He was himself completely exhausted and quite clearly on the verge of death, but he still kept protecting his shipmate with the last of his strength."

He coughed, as though to hide his feelings, then took another sip from his glass. "It was one of the bravest things I've ever heard of," he said. "He got the VC for that, you know," then added as though they might not have understood. "The Victoria Cross. That is the highest honour anyone can achieve in war. Only the very best get that distinction, and then only for exceptional valour."

The others around the table, stirred uncomfortably and looked at each other, their drinks long forgotten. "Do you know what the sad part was?" the older man asked. Their faces remained blank, so he told them. "The shipmate Jack fought to save in those cold waters had already been dead for two days before they were found."

He shook his head sadly, then added, "Three months later he was back on the subs, and stayed there for the duration. That took a lot of guts after what he had been through!"

The old man paused, then mumbled, "For some reason they called their craft the yellow submarine, but I have no idea why."

He emptied the last drops of gin from his glass, and got up. "The bravest man I ever knew," he repeated, then nodded to them and walked away.

Do you Remember, Do you Recall 1961

- Cuban exiles supported by CIA attempted an invasion of Cuba at Bay of Pigs to overthrow Fidel Castro, with embarrassing results for the US government
- The Berlin Wall was finished. Eight feet of concrete that tore a nation apart and destroyed familes living there. The Wall of Shame was a fitting description.
- Adolf Eichmann was sentenced to death in Jerusalem and hanged.
- Clark Gable, the only Rhett Butler there could be, Gone With the Wind.
- Writer Ernest Hemingway died in the only way he could; with a gun in his hand.
- John Wayne fought to save the Alamo, but lost the battle just like Davy Crockett before him.
- Elegant David Niven, sturdy Gregory Peck, volatile Anthony Quinn, and our very own Welsh hero Stanley Baker braved the waves and the nazis to destroy The Guns of Navarone

Some popular records of the year that went right to the top:
- Are You Lonesome Tonight: Elvis making an old classic his very own
- Sailor: Sweet Petula Clark making us all join in
- Walking Back to Happiness: Please don't treat Helen Shapiro like a child, (Whompa Oh Yeh Yeh)
- Runaway: Del Shannon with the falsetto in his tonsils.

"Those were the days my friend, we thought they'd never end ..."
Those Were the Days (Raskin)
Mary Hopkin 1968

at my age? She chuckled to herself, then corrected herself; *especially* at my age!

For some reason, as though conjured forth from nothing, figures gradually began to fill her mind. Some were talking, others dancing, and the picture slowly took shape filling out with the interior surrounding them; paintings hanging on the walls, colourful draperies, tall windows reaching almost to the ceiling, tables with bottles and glasses on them. There was a wide, curved and carpeted staircase along one wall climbing to the floor above, and there was a band playing from a small stage, and she was suddenly there, in the picture, being led towards the dance-floor, and she watched as Peter, as handsome as he had ever been, swept her into his arms and led her in the dance.

Other couples were dancing around them, but they were no more than shadows, and she hardly noticed them, only following the movement of Peter and the woman in his arms as they glided across the floor seeming not to touch it. Her mouth moved silently to the music she could hear in her mind accompanying them, and her head swayed to the rhythm as though she was still there in his arms.

The clock on the sideboard struck a note and the picture immediately melted away, gone. She sighed, and took the cushion from her back and patted it back to shape, then replaced it where it had been.

The war had changed many things, but most of all it had opened society to pleasure and freedom, introducing the youth of the day to a whole new world. It had been an exciting time. A time for youthful exuberance, a time to rid themselves of the inhibitions that had held them back, and allow themselves to become whoever they felt they were inside, and to do whatever they felt that their inclination indicated.

She had done the unthinkable.

Much to her parents' consternation, she had decided to become a writer, and had moved to London to follow her dream. There, she had soon become a part of the environment in which young artists, poets and writers worked and argued, drank and fought, and loved and lived in optimistic poverty, encouraging each other, criticising each other, and supporting each other as best they could, while they hid gnawing doubts behind the pretence of indisputable faith in their own particular talent, and confidence in what the future held for them.

A few were already quite famous in their own sphere, and would sit in attendance, allowing themselves to be applauded for their successes. Some few others would eventually also find some degree of success, but for most of them, only failure and disappointment followed them through their lives.

It had been a fantastic and inspiring time, and she had loved every moment of it and every aspect; the freedom to say what you felt, to do what you wanted to do, and to fall in love and allow yourself to be in love in every way and show it to the whole world, with not a word of criticism or rancour.

They had been politically active young people. She recalled how their frequent discussions, in which they solved all the world's problems, would often become quite heated and could last until the early hours of the morning. She smiled at the memory, and the folly of youth and its insistence that the world could be changed in a moment. She shook her head. No patience, she thought. No patience … We were no better ourselves, she acknowledged with a glimt in her eye.

They had worked together, and had sought and got inspiration from each other. They had worked and they had argued. They had worked and they had fought. They worked and drank. Probably too much, she thought. Somehow a glass was never far away whether they were working or relaxing. Somehow the two seemed to be a part of each other, blending together in an exciting and stimulating mix that gave invigorating life to each new day, and making it whole.

They had been Bohemians before anyone even knew the word. Free spirits and free minds.

None of her work had ever been published, but she had at least had the guts to break out and try to accomplish what she wanted. To fulfill her dreams. She had tried, and that was what mattered. She had failed, but she had at least tried. And had a damned good time doing it, she muttered to herself.

Those were the days, she thought, and sighed again. Who would believe it to look at me now?

She heard a key turning the lock in the front door, and a voice calling, "Mum, it's only me!" and she came awake feeling the pleasure of company arriving. "Come in, Eileen," she said, as she walked towards the door with a welcoming smile on her face.

The daughter was a grown woman, exactly half her own age. At forty she reminded her of herself when she had been forty years younger; the same nose and the same eyes. Others in the family claimed not to be able to see the resemblance, but she saw it clearly. Eileen had children of her own, too quickly growing into adults – how time passes, she thought, whenever she saw them – and she could also see some of herself in them.

The teapot came on the table, the biscuits were taken from the tin, and they talked as they drank their tea and nibbled their biscuits. They talked of present-day problems and gossiped about people they knew. They touched on family, and brought some happy events from their past into the conversation. "You remember uncle Malcolm, don't you?" Eileen did, and yes, she also remembered when he had lost his dentals while singing the high notes of *O Sole Mio* late in the evening at her sister's wedding twenty odd years ago. They laughed at the memory, then sat in silent reflection.

"That was in nineteen sixty one," her mother said. "Can you believe it?"

There was a long pause as they both settled on their own particular thoughts, allowing them time to enfold.

"That was a good time, that was," Eileen broke the silence. "The Beatles and all that stuff," she reminded her mother. "That was when it all started," she said. "That's when we changed the world."

She laughed. "Turned it upside down we did, and it was never the same again!"

She took a sip of tea, and her eyes became distant. "I went to school with George," she said, as though her mother hadn't heard it before. "He was a nice lad".

For a moment she was no longer in the sitting room with her mother, but back twenty years in time when she had still been a young girl learning the game and enjoying the lesson. She remembered the Cavern and the Iron Door Club, and all the dance halls that used to be, but no longer were, and she sighed as the memories came back to her.

Overnight, dirty old Liverpool had become exciting and vibrating. The navel of the world. And she had been there. A part of it. The lunchtime sessions at the Cavern when you queued up along Mathew Street waiting to pay your one and sixpence to pass Paddy the bouncer on the door and climb down those grotty dark stairs to the heaven below that had sweat coming out of its armpits. And there to enjoy the excitement and fun of two hours with the Beatles as they bantered them from the small stage, joking with them, and playing two solid hours of music that made you feel so good as you eventually climbed back to the almost fresh air of the street.

If it wasn't them, then Gerry would be there with his band. Or the Big Three, or one of the other groups. They were all great, but none could compare with George and the lads.

She remembered that they had had two microphones; one for the song's lead singer, and the other shared by the other two as they chanted their replies to whatever the first was singing. And Ritchie on the drums, driving the rhythm home with a content smile on his face, after Pete had had to go.

She must have heard them play a hundred times, she thought. At least!

Twice they had driven her home in the van after a dance. "Can't have you walking around on your own at this time of night, Eileen," Paul had told her, and they had driven her home. The fee the first time had been a friendly kiss for each of them. Nothing more. Just a quick peck on the lips – they were nice lads and were just being friendly. The second time, George had walked with her to the door and given her a real goodnight kiss.

"God love us!" she thought, "Imagine that happening today!"

She had mentioned it once or twice when talking with people she knew today, but she was certain that they didn't believe her. But who cares? she thought, I was there, and it was me he was kissing! and she smiled at the memory.

They had never been more than friends. She had never loved any of them, but she had loved them all – like most of the girls who saw them play.

There was something indescribable in the air in those days. Something exciting. Something that told them that, Hey! You can do it too! Whatever you want, just go for it! And it had opened their minds and their ambitions, and made them want to *try*.

It had been a fantastic time.

Being young, she acknowledged, is always a fantasy, but this … well, this was something special. Something we will never experience again. So hold on to the memories, girl, she thought. Keep them safe!

As though coming out of a trance, she looked around her and was once more back again in her mother's living room. "Those were the days," she said wistfully, and took a sip from the cup in her hand.

Her mother glanced at her, then let her eyes rest on the flowery wallpaper. She sighed quietly. "Yes," she whispered, "Those were the days …"

"I'm drowning my sorrows in whisky and gin …"
Death of a Clown (Davies/Davies)
Dave Davies 1967

Death of a Clown

"You've been drinking again!" The words came before the ringmaster had climbed the steps into the worn caravan. He lowered his head to avoid the ceiling as he came through the door, and scowled at the figure sitting slumped on the small sofabed, "I told you I wouldn't have it anymore. Damnit, I told you!"

The figure before him had turned at the sound of his voice, and the anxiety in his eyes showed through the grotesque make-up he wore on his face. He opened his mouth to respond but the ringmaster broke him off before he could speak. "It won't do! I'm not running a frigging home for drunks and alcoholics. This is a circus for christ's sake!" He leaned against the small cupboard and stared down at the man before him. "This is the last time Joey. I mean it. The last time, you hear!"

Behind the mask of make-up the clown understood, but his mind defended himself "I'm not drunk Mr. Davies, honest." As he said it, he wondered if it was true. "I only had one drink." This was a lie, and they both knew it. He noticed the glass on the table before him, and quietly moved it, hoping to hide it from the other man's view.

The ringmaster shook his head and sighed, then lowered himself to sit on the bed next to the clown. His anger had subsided and he now felt some pity for the pathetic creature sitting next to him. He still had the wig and funny hat on his head. A big round, red nose dominated the painted face.

41

The clown still wore the clothes he had worn during the show, and he hadn't bothered to take off the enormous clown shoes that reached across the small passage in the camper where he sat.

Under the circumstances it seemed ludicrous to talk about something so serious, but the ringmaster tried. He had had the same conversation before, not just with Joey the clown, although this was by no means the first time he had tried to get through to him, but also other artistes (he always called them "artistes", never "artists" – it came with the job). They had all found that the boredom and loneliness of touring with a small circus could be alleviated with the contents of a bottle.

"There are kids out there, Joey," he began. "Do you know who they've come to see?" He raised his eyebrows in question. There was no response, but he continued as though there had been. "That's right, Joey," he nodded his head. "They've come to see the clowns." His voice was reasonable and explanatory as though he was talking to a child. "They've come to see you." He pointed at him. "You, Joey. You."

The clown's hands hung in the opening between the baggy, chequered trouser legs, his head was lowered and his shoulders slumped. Behind the mask, his face was haggard and drawn, and he stared in silence at the dirty cheap carpet on the floor, without seeing it. He was only half listening as the ringmaster droned on. A picture came into his mind. A woman and a little girl. They weren't doing anything. They weren't smiling or crying or talking. They were just there, in his mind. Then they were gone.

It seemed to have happened just as quickly when she had left him and taken their daughter from him nine years earlier. She had just said that she had had enough, and gone. In a way he could understand her, but he didn't think he had deserved her leaving him like that, and he had never come over it. He had never seen either of them again, and missed them terribly. At each new show in each new town he would search the faces in the crowd hoping to see them. But he never did.

She had expected more of him, and he had led her to believe that he would fulfill her expectancies, because he too believed that he would succeed in his ambition to make a living as a comedian in showbusiness. Christ, everybody said he was funny … They always had. "You should be on the stage, Joey, you're a bloody comedian, you are …" How many times he had heard that through the years, and how often he had wanted to believe it so much that, in the end, he did. He had always made people laugh, so why shouldn't he go for it?

He had started doing turns in pubs and clubs where the beer flowed freely and the public were enthusiastic. He loved the response from the audience and the sound of the laughter, and was always exhilarated when his turn was over and he left the stage to the sound of applause. It gave him an indescribable feeling of joy that lasted for hours. Eventually an agent had signed him. He was not a good agent, but the work increased and he got better bookings with more money.

"I'm going to make it Suzie," he had told her. "Just wait and see." And she had believed him.

As he gradually became better-known, the bookings took him further afield, and after some time he found himself travelling throughout the country, with only the odd day to spend at home. Things were looking up. They were married on the day of his first television appearance – two reasons to celebrate what was to be the start of a new life. He had felt that he deserved the happiness of marriage with the woman he loved, but even more, he felt that he deserved the success that they both now felt was within their grasp.

He had a certain fame. His name was becoming quite well known, and he was making a good living. He was far from rich, but they had enough to get by on, and his prospects were looking good. He thrived on the applause and the laughter, and felt immense pride knowing that he was in such demand, and that people wanted to see and hear him. Although he was not yet a star, he felt that he was on the way to becoming one, and life was good. They took a mortgage and bought a nice house, and nine months later, their daughter was born. Yes, life was good …

His agent died in a road accident three years later. Although he had managed to get him better bookings that had helped his career, he had never been a good agent. Nonetheless, it turned out that he had been a better agent than a caretaker of the funds he had accumulated on behalf of his client. Everything was gone. On high costs and bad investments. There was nothing left. The assets that had been built up on his behalf, through six hard and successful years of touring, were all gone.

They had had to sell the house. Suzie had been furious, but he had calmed her with assurances that he would be making new money, and that things would work out. He had been stunned by the money that was gone, and saddened at the loss of their home, but he still felt optimistic and confident that this was just a temporary setback, and that things would soon be as before.

But he had been wrong.

It didn't happen overnight. It came gradually, but he soon felt it. He still had work, but new comedians with new material had entered the competition. The clubs were also closing down to make way for shopping centres and other developments, so there were now more acts competing for fewer venues, and each appearance became less lucrative than it had been before. His name still gave him a head start, but that alone was not enough to pay the bills and keep the life-style that he had promised Suzie, and to which she had become accustomed.

Slowly but surely times became harder. His name didn't carry the same weight that it had done before. Although he still did the pubs and the odd show at one of the few remaining clubs, there was never enough money. Suzie had demanded that he get a job. "Get a job, for christs sake!" she had repeated so often that it hurt him to hear her say it. "We need the bloody money!" As if he didn't know. But how could he take a job? He was Joey Jam, the comedian. Everybody knew him. He'd been on the tele, for gods sake! How was he supposed to drive a bus or work in a shop!! He'd be the laughing stock of everybody who saw him! He wanted to make people laugh, but not like that!

Then she left him. Just like that. One day here, the next, gone. And he never saw her again.

He felt disillusioned and ridiculed. All the optimism that had earlier held him up and driven him forward, was gone, now replaced by pessimism and apathy that held him down and drew him deeper into melancholy and depression. The comedian no longer laughed, but the tears were apparent for all to see. He loathed himself for what he had become and for what he had lost, and for the situation in which he found himself. He couldn't face the prospect of meeting people. They would expect to see the flamboyant comedian that he had once been, the famous face with the funny wisecracks who had been so successful. Instead they would only see a sad and lonely figure with no money and no family, a disillusioned and pathetic failure. But he still needed to earn money to survive.

That was when he decided to become a clown.

Then he could hide behind the mask and nobody would see his misery. Nobody would recognise him for the man he had once been. He could start a new life and still hear the laughter, without himself needing the pretence of a smile that he no longer wore on his face. No one would be able to see the pain behind the painting on his face. In the circus he would have a home again, and an income, and he would be able to hide behind the mask of a clown.

The drinking began slowly. First, after the last show. Then, also between shows. Now, he drank when it suited him. He had never felt it to be a problem. Quite the contrary; he felt that it helped him through the long days and the lonely nights, and loosened him up to face the audiences when he would hear the children laughing at him excitedly. Whereas the laughter of the audience had once exhilarated him, it now only made him sad, reminding him, as it did, of his earler life. But now he had been caught again, and threatened with the sack. What was he to do if he was sacked? He didn't know. There were always other circuses, he told himself … But he didn't know. Or care. Life was meaningless anyway.

The sound of the ringmaster's voice penetrated his thoughts again. "So no more drinking on the job, eh?" He got to his feet and looked down at the figure slumped before him on the sofabed. "I'm glad we had this talk, Joey," he said. "I know I can rely on you, so please, no more booze." The clown raised his face slowly and looked at him without a word. The ringmaster took this as a confirmation. "Right, then," he said, "I'll see you tomorrow." He went outside and closed the door behind him, leaving the clown alone with his thoughts.

He sat for a long time without moving, then reached out and flipped open the cupboard door. A bottle of gin stared at him from a shelf. He stared back for long moments, then slowly pulled the red nose from his face, and reached for it.

Martha, the fortune teller, found him the next morning. Although her clairvoyance was as false as the eyelashes she wore, she had had an uneasy feeling that brought her to his caravan that morning. There was no reply to her knock, so she opened the door and went inside.

He was lying on top of the sofa bed with his arms crossed over his chest as though asleep. He still wore the mask on his face, and the clown's clothes. The stupid shoes on his feet reached towards the ceiling, almost touching it. He held the big, red nose in one hand, and an empty pill glass in the other, and he was dead.

She found a piece of paper on the table under the empty bottle, and turned it over. "Isn't life a laugh?" she read. "Ha! Ha! Ha!" She smothered a tear, then climbed out of the caravan, calling to those around her, "The clown's dead!" She swallowed to contain herself, then repeated, "Joey's dead, poor bugger. The clown's dead!" Then she cried.

Do you Remember, Do you Recall **1962**

- The Cuban crisis, with the Russians shipping in rockets and the Americans setting up a blockade to stop them. Eyeball to eyeball, Kennedy called Nikita's bluff and won the poker pot, while the rest of the world held its collective breath and thought the 3rd. World War was about to happen.
- Marilyn Monroe was found dead in her home, 36 years old. We never quite believed that she wasn't helped on her way by others, and some of us still don't. With such powerful friends as the Kennedys, who needs enemies?
- The Beatles made their first chart entry with Love Me Do – and we did!
- Charlton Heston played Ben Hur, and Benny stayed with him for the rest of his life (It was a long film).
- Elvis played Elvis, this time in Blue Hawaii, with a ukelele in his hand – and why not …?
- Hitchcock let Anthony Perkins run loose in a motel with his old Mom, much to the distress of Janet Leigh and the audiences. What a Psycho!!
- Dr. No. Sean Connery introduced himself "My name's Bond. James Bond." He was!

Some popular records of the year that went right to the top:
- The Young Ones: Cliff Richard never got older, did he?
- Good Luck Charm: Elvis – uh, uh, uh, uh, uh, uh, uh, uh, uh, oh yeh – Fantastic lyrics!
- I Remember You: Frank Ifield (The good-looking guy with the smile and the yodel).

"… said little boy, I'm gonna make you a man …"
Lola (Davies)
The Kinks 1970

Lola

"IT'S PARTY TIME!!!"

He stood by the table and held his glass high, as he shouted it out with his head held back.

"YEAHHH!!!" the others sang out, as they too got to their feet and shook their heads exhuberantly as though they were Beatles in a concert. They downed their beer and slapped the glasses on the table, then went towards the door of the pub as they howled like wolves, whooped and laughed, and slapped each other on the back in camaraderie and encouragement.

It was another Saturday night and they'd just got paid …

Now they were going to get laid. Or die trying.

They had been drinking for a few hours, moving from one pub to the next, and feeling their inhibitions easing with each new drink they had. They were in a good mood. No, they were in a fantastic mood! It was Saturday night, for christs sake, and the whole world was their oyster! Who could tell how the night would end? And in the meantime, they were having a hell of a time, looking forward with excited expectancy, to whatever the next hours would offer them.

They were four friends in their early twenties, with no other commitment than to devour life. It was Saturday night - their night - and they owned the world. It was theirs for the taking!

The music from Merseyside had opened the door, and the kids were now raring and raw, as they had never been before, and the four friends were all twentyfour, and no different from any of the millions of young people who had finally ripped open the shutters and shaken off the shackles of the fifties, to live their lives as they pleased, and to seek their destinies wherever they might be found.

Their lives had revolved around Saturday nights since they had been old enough to drink. It had kept them going through the dreary weeks of working at the factory that gave them enough money to pay their keep, with enough left over to let them live their lives in the weekend. The weekends that they impatiently waited for during the rest of the week, when they had to hold back the simmering energy that was only waiting to explode with the possibilities that life offered them when Friday finally came.

Some had had short-lived romances lasting a week or a month, but when they had got a girl interested, it usually only lasted for a day or two. Or just the night. Just a one night stand. Yet that was enough. They had got their beans, and could take their eggs with breakfast, feeling good. Feeling good! They had then again proved their manhood, and enjoyed the experience, swaggering towards their friends the next day with a fist in the air, as though to say, "Yeah, another one under the belt!" and enjoying the adulation and the frenetic questions that followed, "What happened? What did you do? What was she like?" Then telling them …

One of the friends had once claimed to have got the clap from one of the Saturday night conquests, and his friends had hung on every word as he told of his experiences at the local hospital. "They poked a fucking needle up my dick," he had told them, "and it hurt like hell." Then he had smirched, "But it was bloody worth it!" He had rolled his eyes as he added, "You wouldn't have believed those tits."

Then he had got the clap again, and his friends had been even more impressed, as though this somehow confirmed his sexual prowess, and he had risen even higher in their esteem.

Another had held them in agonising suspense for three weeks after he had told them that one of his conquests had informed him that she was pregnant. In those days a pregnancy meant marriage, whether you wanted it or not. "She was crying her bloody eyes out when she told me," he had said. "She really wanted me, and she wanted me to marry her, poor cow." He had looked at the others, and meant it when he had said, "She was only a scrubber. A quickie after the dance in Manchester. You remember. Josie!" He had shrugged his shoulders as if to say, "So what!?" then added, "Anyway, she was half pissed herself when I got her knickers off," as though that excused him from responsibility.

As it happened, it had been a false alarm, and he could relax and enjoy the prospects of new conquests. And there were many waiting for him.

But, among the four friends, it was acknowledged that it was George who had the magic touch. The others rolled their eyes in admiration at his exploits, because he scored every weekend. New girls, sometimes a grown woman, and once even a married woman he had led from a club to give her the goods that she never got from her old man. He had told them the stories but, as opposed to his friends, he had always left out the juicy bits. But that only made them even more exciting in their minds, where their imaginations sensually lived out what he had withheld from them.

They were in no doubt. He was the king. He got the women, and he got them whenever he wanted them. Then left them as quickly as he had found them. Whereas they sometimes missed out, he scored every time. Every weekend. Every Saturday, and any time at all, he got what he wanted.

They were his pals, and they were impressed, and he enjoyed every word that underlined the awe they expressed for the conquests he had made, and for the obvious sexual attraction that brought them to him.

But nothing was true. He had never had a woman, although he had tried a hundred times, and wanted nothing more than to feel their embrace and explore the mysteries that they represented. But he had never experienced the warmth, the heat, the passion, and he had no idea how to unleash them to his own satisfaction. He was a virgin, and despised himself for it. He felt guilty remorse for feeding his friends false lies to make them believe that he was a conqueror, a king, and that women fell at his feet, when he himself knew the sad truth, that he had never once been in a woman's sexual embrace.

Once, in sheer desperation, he had gone with a prostitute, but it had been a sad and seedy experience. "Never mind, love," she had said in a bored voice, as he quickly pulled on his clothes to escape. "It'll work out next time." His friends considered him a king, but he knew he was a helpless loser, and he felt the burden of his lies weighing heavily on his shoulders.

But there was always hope and new possibilities and, as they now hit the street with beer in the belly and fire in the loins, roaring into the darkness of another Saturday night, he felt lucky. The hunt was on!

The first club was throbbing with loud music and shouting voices competing for attention while the revellers pushed against each other as they moved through the crowd between the bars and the dancefloor. Getting a girl's attention was as difficult as movement, and keeping it was almost impossible. After balancing a couple of drinks to avoid spilling them as people milled around them, they decided to move on, and entered another club a few minutes walk away.

The entrance was illuminated with coloured, blinking lights, and they could hear the sound of music and laughter coming from inside. Although they had never been there before, they felt drawn towards it, and moved up the stone steps to pass the bouncer on the door and pay their money to the woman behind the counter.

They peered into the dimly lit club within the inner doors, and felt an expectancy growing in them. "This looks allright, doesn't it?" one said excitedly, as they stared into the activities inside. The others nodded without saying anything, then they moved through the doors looking right and left as they crossed to a bar, inhaling the atmosphere of the place with wide-eyed anticipation. This was more like it! There were birds all over the place, just ripe for the plucking, and they were ready and willing to do the job!

As their eyes became accustomed to the darkness, they noticed the eyes looking at them. Some with casual interest, others lazily loitering on them, while others again blatantly stared at them with no signs of embarrassment. One of the friends showed his teeth in an exaggerated smile of withheld energy, nudged George, and chuckled "We're going to be allright here!" and they laughed in anticipation of what the night might offer.

They began the game, chatting up the women around them, buying them drinks and taking them on the dancefloor, then moving on to another woman when they felt that their chances might prove better there. George bought another drink and stood by the bar watching his friends moving to the music each with a girl in his arms, stroking them to test the response, as they joked and laughed with them.

"Are you new here?" It was a husky voice.

He turned around and found himself looking into the face of a stunning redhead smiling at him with a sweet smile on her face. Even through the smoke and the sweat of a hundred bodies, he could smell her perfume. He glanced around to see who she was talking to, then turned back to her as he realised that it was him. "What do you mean?" he asked, flustered.

"Is this your first time here?" she said, "Have you been here before?"

"No. This is the first time," he managed to reply, and didn't know how to continue.

The redhead didn't seem to notice his discomfort, and held his eyes as she casually continued, "You'll like it." His heart jumped as his sex-fixated mind chose the sexual innuendo that the words could have implied. She studied him for a moment without speaking, as though making up her mind, then told him "My name's Charlotte, but everyone calls me Lola." The music became louder so she leaned her mouth next to his ear. "What's yours?"she asked, and he felt her breath tickle against his neck, making his whole body shivver with anticipation. He told her. "Do you want to dance?" she asked him, then took his hand and led him to the floor before he could answer.

The way she had taken the initiative was spellbinding. Nothing like this had ever happened to him before. He was used to being the hunter, chasing the girls with his tongue hanging out, and here he was, trapped by a woman who obviously fancied him and wasn't afraid to show it. And what a woman! A bit older than him. Late thirties, he guessed, but so what? She was sexy and she was hot, and she scared the shit out of him, but he wasn't going to let a chance like this slip away.

As the evening wore on, his apprehension eased as they talked. He felt more comfortable in her company for each hour that passed. She was easy to talk to and fun to be with, and he gradually felt relaxed in her company, enjoying himself more than he could remember. He found that he was able to talk openly with her in a way that he had never been able to do with anyone before, even with his best friends.

He made no attempt at physical contact although he felt her attraction pressing against his pants, and felt the excitement when she placed her hand on his thigh and squeezed it gently, somehow making it seem completely natural instead of the obvious invitation it was meant to be. She gave him a kiss, uninvited and unexpected. It thrilled him, and he responded with such eagerness that she pulled away from him, laughing. "Not here, darling," she said, then took his hand and looked deeply into his eyes, "Let's go to my place." So they did.

He could hardly keep his hands off her as they sat in the back of the taxi that took them to her flat, and he could feel the desire building up inside him. When they got there, he was ready to burst and wanted to be inside her as soon as the door closed, but she firmly, and good naturedly, eased him away from her and into a sofa. "Relax, we've got all night," she told him. "This is going to be so nice, just wait and see."

She lowered the lights and put on some music, then brought them each a glass of red wine, and slid into the sofa close to him as she murmured, "Take your time George, this is going to be so good." He made a new attempt, but was again held off, so he gradually eased off to wait for her to take an initiative, knowing that it would come.

"Are you still a virgin, George?" she asked so innocently, that he really didn't mind the question, however unexpected it was. Normally he would have refuted such an accusation as being laughable, but looking into her knowing eyes, he only hesitated for a moment before admitting it. "Yes," he answered honestly, "I am." He put on a wry smile as he tried to deflate it with a joke "I've been a virgin all my life .."

Instead of feeling embarrassed by his revelation, he felt relief. He also felt the throbbing in his groin increasing, as though by having admitted his innocence to the beautiful and sexy woman beside him, he had paid the price for whatever came next. He had now thrown off whatever shackles of inhibition that had held him back in earlier and failed attempts to lose the burden of virginity, and he knew he was now about to lose it to this exciting woman.

He noticed the pupils of her eyes inflate at his confession, and saw the desire in them as they again settled on him. She took the glass from his hand and placed it with her own on the table. "Just relax, George," her husky voice whispered, as her hand crept to loosen his belt, "and leave it all to me .." Then she took control.

He was soon lying naked on the sofa, writhing with the pleasure he felt, and he clumsily began to loosen her dress, wanting her naked body next to his. Wanting to hold and touch it, and feel himself inside her. Instead, she gently removed his groping hands, and in a few practiced movements removed her clothes without leaving his body. She then pressed herself against him as he let out an ecstatic moan at the feel of her flesh.

Moments passed in heated contact, then he heard his own voice gasping out in shocked surprise, "What the fuck???!!!" and he shoved her off him, and crawled out of the sofa staggering to his feet as he stared in amazement and disgust at the man climbing to his feet from the floor where he had fallen.

He shook his head as if this was a nightmare he had just woken from. His disbelief stared from his face in shock and despair, and sounds came from somewhere deep in his throat, then he lashed out and hit the naked man in the face, so he fell with a cry of pain and fear, then lay cowering on the floor expecting another attack.

George hovered over him, his mind in turmoil, then became aware of his own nakedness and his rapidly shrivelling manhood. Tears came to his eyes. He felt the bile coming and threw up on the sofa where he had experienced such unknown ecstacy only moments earlier. He ran to the bathroom and found a towel, then feverishly began to wash himself, as though the harder he scrubbed the more of his shame could be rubbed away. He then went back into the lounge and dressed quickly, keeping his eyes from her. He corrected himself with an oath. Him! Him, for christs sake! Him!

He slammed the door behind him as he left, and could just make out the sound of stifled whimpering before the door slammed shut.

He kept to himself the next week. When he met his friends at work, he stayed quiet when they asked him how his night had been; if he had got lucky. Their own bragging only brought the embarrassment of his own miserable experience back to him in force, and for the first time, he reacted to their detailed, smirking, brags with disgust. It was all so meaningless. So false. So empty. He wondered if there had ever been any truth in what they said, or if their lives were also as miserable as his own. If they were just compensating for their own disappointments with illusions and lies that they wanted to believe were true, but knew to be false.

As time went by, he found himself reviewing the life he had led with his friends, and realised its waste. They were aimlessly living a lie, with no real content or aims to their lives. He couldn't even be honest with them. Although they were his best friends, he still had to hide in pretence to avoid them seeing who he really was.

He remembered how good it had felt to be able to openly admit that he was a virgin. To Lola. He gritted his teeth at the name and the memory, but both kept coming back to him. More often as the weeks passed, and the initial shock and disgust had subsided. He had really liked her, he admitted. She had been fun to be with and he had really felt comfortable with her. More comfortable than with his friends, he realised wryly. He felt despondent and lonely, and wondered if he was gay, but knew that he wasn't. So why did he keep thinking of her?

It was another Saturday night, and he still had nobody. Now he didn't even have his friends around him anymore. It was dark and cold outside, and he had his hands deep in his coat pockets to keep them warm as he walked up the steps and entered the club. He saw the red hair among the crowd by the bar, and walked over.

"Hello, Lola," he said, uncertainly, "I'm really sorry …"

Do you Remember, Do you Recall 1963

- The Profumo affair – And what an affair! Christine Keeler, Mandy Rice-Davis, a Russian diplomat (read spy!) and poor old John. He just had to go! And he did …
- So did Harold Macmillan. And why not? Everybody was doing it …
- The Great Train Robbery didn't do anyone any good except Phil Collins, who later got a good part in a film because of it.
- The Pill!!! At last a bit of peace of mind when we had fornication in mind.
- A flustered Bamber Gascoigne broke into his live tv-show to tell us that President John F. Kennedy had just been shot in Dallas.
- Lee Harvey Oswald, the lone assassin, was killed by Jack Ruby two days later. Lone assassin? Of course he was alone! After all it's not that difficult to hit a moving target in the head with three shots in the space of a few seconds. And why shouldn't the bullets have come from various directions? Come on … Why make a problem of it …!
- Peter Sellers and James Mason chased little schoolgirls in Lolita
- Peter O'Toole chased the Turks on the back of a camel in Lawrence of Arabia
- Marlon Brando chased the Pacific for a bit on the side in Mutiny on the Bounty
- The Germans chased Steve McQueen on his motorbike in The Great Escape

Some popular records of the year that went right to the top:
- Summer Holiday: Cliff Richard and the Shadows getting some sun
- How Do You Do It: Gerry & The Pacemakers with the song the Beatles didn't want
- She Loves You: The Beatles with the one that really started it all – yeah, yeah, yeah!
- Sweets For My Sweet: The Searchers with their own particular sound

"Day after day alone on the hill …
The Fool on the Hill (Lennon/McCartney)
The Beatles "Magical Mystery Tour" 1967

The Fool on the Hill

The man wandered back and forth behind the French windows of the living room like a cat in a cage, with his head down and deep in thought. Sometimes he would stop pacing the floor and stand looking through the glass, staring down the valley that lay green and fertile below him. From the house on the low hill he could see for miles around him, from the village that nestled harmoniously at the foot of the hill to the town that somehow kept creeping closer year by year.

He placed his hands behind his back as he began to pace the floor once more, backwards and forwards before the French windows, as though it was some kind of ritual. He stopped and raised his head to gaze at the ceiling for a moment, then walked quickly through a door into another room and sat down by an old mahogany desk. Before him was a typewriter, with a sheet of paper in it. He looked at it, then rolled the paper down a line and began to type.

He lived alone in his thatched cottage and had no contact with others. The milkman and the paperboy who called early in the morning would see him through the windows pacing backwards and forwards through the living room. And the postman who called a little later in the day would see the same thing. But he had never had reason to speak to them, and these were the only visitors he ever had. Actually this was not quite true, because a car would wind its way up the path to the cottage once or twice a year, and would then leave again a few hours later.

The villagers would then have reason to speculate on who the visitor might have been, because nobody ever visited the cottage on the hill. Some thought that it might be some fancy woman up from London to remind him of what life was all about. Others thought that he might have become ill and had called a doctor. At this, the regulars in the pub would laugh and say, "More likely a psychiatrist. They'll be taking him away any day now, and about time too!"

The fact that he kept to himself confounded the people of the village, but also tittilated their curiosity, and the machinations of their minds would sometimes run wild. That he was living the life of a hermit, alone among people, was in itself a contradiction, but the fact that nobody knew him, who he was, or where he had come from, made him the natural focus of interest for the villagers and the other inhabitants of the valley.

On the rare occasions when he walked down the path to the village, they would stop whatever they were doing and follow his movements. They never saw him well dressed. On the contrary, he always looked rather shabby, as though he had just got out of bed. He seemed not to notice them as he passed by them, seeming to be preoccupied with his own thoughts. Sometimes a villager would point to his own head and make circular motions with a finger after he had passed by, to indicate his personal diagnosis of the man, while the hermit continued on his way, unaware of the people following him with their eyes and inquisitive minds.

These visits were only and always to buy groceries. He would pick out what he needed and pay what was required of him, murmur "Thank you," then wander back the way he had come, just as preoccupied as before. The visits to the village lasted no more than twenty minutes, and only occurred twice a week; Tuesday and Friday, as regular as clockwork. They would see him coming, expecting him, they would see him leaving, and then he was gone again, as great an enigma as he had been before.

He had arrived at the village seventeen years earlier. A removal van had arrived and had wound its way up the path to the cottage, and the villagers had watched with surprise as the few possessions were carried inside. They noticed a bed, a sideboard, a table and a few chairs carried in, then a few crates followed, before the van returned down the path and drove away through the valley. Hardly what was necessary to furnish a home, they had thought, and began to wonder who the new inhabitant was to be. They hadn't even seen a television being carried in! And true enough, an aerial never appeared on the roof of the cottage. So whatever did he do with his time? They had no idea, and that only served to increase their speculative interest in the new inhabitant of the cottage on the hill.

The local vicar and one or two other local dignitaries took it upon themselves to pay him a visit, in the belief that they might help him to adjust to his new environment by inviting him to various social gatherings that they were to hold. However, they had come away with their ambitions unfulfilled, yet assuring whoever might ask, that they had been welcomed and as well treated as could be expected, but that he had nonetheless been less than forthcoming and politely non-commital to their approaches.

As the years passed, the villagers became accustomed to having a mysterious hermit as a neighbour, but their curiosity never waned, although their early conviction that he was "special", gradually increased to "eccentric", before finally ending in the conclusion that they had a "weirdo" as a neighbour. Being country people, they never went further than this, although many felt that he must be a simpledon and, in general conversation, came to refer to him as the fool on the hill.

After the initial attempts to bring him into the community had failed, no others were made. It was up to him, they thought. If he wants to be alone, then let him. So they did.

Some felt sympathy for him. After all it couldn't be much of a life living on his own and never seeing anyone, never having anybody to talk to. "No wonder he's bonkers," one said, "He's got no life."

But she was wrong.

The fool on the hill lived a secret life that the villagers knew nothing of. It was a life so full of people and places and adventures that it could have filled a dozen lifetimes. He was a magician who could travel the world every day at a whim. Who could create living people of flesh and blood and make them do as he wanted. He could change events or create them as he pleased. He could kill or deceive or make love at his pleasure, and there was no-one to stop him from doing whatever he wanted, because he was God, and he created his own world. Not in the seven days of the First Testament, but every day of the week, and every week of the year.

He was a writer.

While the villagers pitied him for the lonely life he led, his own world was filled to the brim with unbelievable wonders that they could not even envisage. There were no boundaries to his world, no shackles of decorum or religion, rules or regulations, or conformity of any kind.

The possibilities were endless. Only his own mind decided how far he was able to reach into the limitless void that grew out of the world over which he ruled with the aid of creativity and imagination.

The fact that he had no contact with the outside world was of no consequence to him as he had a more vivid and enthralling world in the accesses of his own mind, and shared these with the world outside with the words that he wrote and the books they eventually became.

Their success meant nothing to him. As little as the money he earned from their sales. It was only the process of creation that preoccupied his mind and filled his life. It filled it with new challenges every day, and the excitement of winning over them, forming them to his needs, and seeing them gradually develop and come alive with each new word he wrote on the pages before him.

He would write until he became too tired to continue. Then he would sleep while dreaming of the activities of the characters inhabiting his mind and his world, before he again awoke to tap out their lives, their thoughts and their feelings, on the typewriter, only broken off to intermittently pace the floor of the living room before the French windows, as he pondered their fate. Alone, but far from lonely.

One day a stranger drove into the village. After parking his car he walked into the local pub and ordered a beer. He sipped it gratefully, then asked the publican if he knew where the author lived. The publican scratched his neck, and replied uncertainly. "No authors, hereabouts, sir. Not that I know of."

"I'm a journalist," the stranger explained, "and I've come down to try to get an interview." To help the publican place him, he added, "His name's Peter Blake. He's a famous writer."

The publican shook his head slowly, "No Peter Blake living round here," he said. "I'd know if there was."

The journalist frowned and took another sip of his beer, wondering if he had been directed to the wrong village. "He's a bachelor," he explained. "I believe he lives on his own somewhere around here."

The publican shrugged his shoulders and began to wipe a glass he had taken from the water in the sink. "The only one who lives on his own around here is that old fool on the hill," and he nodded his head towards the window, through which they could see the low hill that rose from the village, "Mr. Jenkins, his name is," he said. "But he's just some old fool." He pointed to the cottage, "Lives up there, he does. In that cottage." Then he shook his head again and assured the journalist, "But he's no author." He gave a short laugh, "He probably can't even write his own name, poor sod."

The journalist thanked the publican for the beer and his attention, and left. The publican's eyes followed him curiously as he walked to the car. He dried off another glass with a frown on his face, thinking, then smiled to himself as he placed it behind the bar. "No," he said, and shook his head. "No way!" He chuckled quietly to himself, then went about his business.

"... All the town's people they boo-booed, now they want to shake his hand ..."
Viva Bobby Joe (Grant)
The Equals 1969

Viva Bobby Joe

Robert Joseph Heaney had been a loser all his life. Or so they kept telling him. His parents and teachers, and everyone who had wanted him to conform, and to accept their discipline and norms. When he failed to do so he would be chided, then told of the consequences of his behaviour to his possibilities, then threatened, and often punished when that was considered to be the only means left at their disposal.

However, none of these managed to change him. No matter what they did, he remained as he was. He had always been independent. He had always questioned the wisdom of authority, just as he had always questioned whatever he had been told. This alone was sometimes enough to cause him problems.

Once at school at the age of twelve, Mr. Burton, the chemistry master, had informed them that $H_2+O_2 = H_2O$. He had been presumptious enough to raise his hand and ask "Why?", much to the irritation of the teacher, who had testily told him, "Because it does!" Not registering the irritation in the voice, and unable to understand, but wanting to, he had repeated the question, "Yes, but why?" and, from that moment on, he had also been termed a trouble-maker in the chemistry class, constantly being punished by Mr. Burton for some assumed misbehaviour.

The teachers knew that he had a high IQ; the tests proved it, but they quite simply didn't like him.

It was certainly not an attempt to disrupt the learning process or cause problems of any kind that had brought him to query the statement of the teacher. It was just how he was. He was inquisitive, wanting to learn why, when, how and where, and how the knowledge could be used to create, to develop and to change. He was also creative enough to allow his dreams to flower, always looking for possibilities, never seeking shelter in realities, but trying to find ways to get around them.

His parents had given him a good home, and never loved him less for his short-comings, but they would often feel dejected and inadequate, wanting him to fulfill the possibilties education could offer him, but unable to make him conform to the necessity of working for it and accepting the framework within which he would have to work if there was to be any hope of succeeding in his endeavours. They often despaired of his lack of will to do so.

He wore his hair long many years before this had become acceptable. He styled his drab school uniform to show who he was, adding various badges and other ornaments to it, much to the chagrine of the school, who wanted no marks of independence showing among their flock. All the pupils were to look alike, work alike, think alike, and achieve alike. But he didn't, and therefore stood out like a sore thumb, to their constant irritation.

Twice he had been expelled from a school. Not for fighting or misbehaviour. Not for disrespect to his teachers, or refusing to do his work. Or any other such valid reason. But simply for refusing to change. For refusing to allow himself to become someone he never was and had no intention of ever becoming. For refusing to be like them. For refusing to be like everyone else. He liked his hair as it was, and did not want it cut short. He felt that the badges and other small ornaments on the school uniform gave him some small identity, and he wanted to keep it. He would always keep questioning facts and figures and whatever he was told, never accepting them until he had been told "Why?" which, to him, was the most important word in his, and any other language.

When he would not conform to their demands, he had simply been re-moved and sent to another school, where the whole process began once again. Even as a boy, Robert Joseph Heaney was a trouble-maker and a loser.

His friend Geoff had a father who ran a newsagency and had more money than many others. They even had a television set when most other families had to content themselves with Billy Cotton or the Goons on the radio. In this particular, he conformed to the majority, and would each week wait impatiently to enjoy the irresistibly irreverent comedy of Peter Sellers, Spike Milligan, Harry Seacombe and the others, with the volume high to catch every ridiculous word as it came through the speaker.

But television had opened his eyes to a new world, and he would always make it a point to be at his friend's house each Sunday evening to be able to see the show from the Palladium, with Tommy Trinder in his hat, joking and introducing the acts that appeared. This was a new and exciting world opening up before his eyes. Popular stars of the day suddenly appeared in the front room and performed for them there.

The turning point for both the boys was when the American star Guy Mitchell came on the stage with a spindleback chair and a box guitar, placed a leg on the chair, rested the guitar on the leg and sang *Singing the Blues* as though just for them. And of course, when Lonnie Donegan came on and showed them what skiffle could do, there was no longer any question of what they wanted.

These two performances alone changed their lives. Suddenly they were only interested in music; listening to it, and making it. Geoff's father had already been paying for his piano lessons for some time, but was now badgered for a guitar, and eventually his father came home with a new one he had bought for him.

The garage was the place. There, they could make as much noise as they wanted to. At least, when the car wasn't there. Geoff would learn one or two chords and use them for all they were worth while he himself hacked at a couple of upturned buckets supposedly keeping rhythm, as they both sang as loudly as they could to hear themselves above the noise they were making. At first there were only two songs they knew the words to, and these were repeated again and again, until they were sick of them, and acquired the words of new songs.

Cumberland Gap and the Guy Mitchell song were soon joined by Tommy Steele and Elvis, and they gradually had enough songs on their repertoire to keep themselves entertained as they enthusiastically destroyed them in the dank confines of the garage.

It was fun and it was exhilarating, a new experience that allowed them to learn as they spent the surplus energy that had to come out some way, and now came out in what they themselves thought to be music. It was a pastime that had taken the place of football and other activities, but which gave them even more pleasure, and they had spent more and more time in the garage, and less time on other activities including homework and other such irrelevancies.

Geoff had quickly taken to the guitar, and could soon play it quite well. This progress had impressed his father to such a degree that he eventually bought him a new one, with a small amplifier. This development not only ensured that the noise they made was better and, perhaps even more important, louder, but it also meant that they now had an extra guitar which he thankfully began to play, gratefully leaving the buckets to their own devises. He was never meant to be a drummer, and the neighbours were undoubtedly as thankful for this admission as he was himself.

"You've got to stop spending so much time with Geoffrey," his parents told him time and again, "and concentrate more on your schoolwork. That's what counts!" He knew they were right and never wanted to disappoint them, but he always found a way to get to the garage.

"Your schoolwork has deteriorated, Heaney," they told him at school. "You will have to pull yourself together if you want to make something of yourself." He knew it had, and he knew he would have to, but his heart wasn't in it, and his mind wandered constantly from the classroom to the present song they were learning, thinking of the chords, the rhythm and the words and how to make them work with just two guitars, one a box-guitar with nylon strings that he couldn't afford to change, and the other, Geoff's electric solo guitar with a quiver that he used whenever he could.

When they had discovered his interest in music they had decided to put him in a class that had extra music lessons, thinking that might stimulate his interest for learning. The idea had some appeal to him at first, but his interest waned quickly as it became apparent that their taste in music was not what appealed to him. *Loch Lomond* may have been a nice enough song, but it hardly compared to Elvis, and *Swanee River* wasn't exactly rivetting. The school was completely out of touch with the times. Whereas Lonnie could excite and inspire, they could not. Quite the opposite! He had been eager to learn and willing to work, but piping away at the recorder was never meant to slake his thirst for making music, and he had quickly lost interest, unable to hide the boredom he felt during classes.

"You're going to be a loser, Heaney!" How many times had they told him the same thing? He was almost beginning to believe it himself. They certainly did! He was fourteen, and already doomed to failure.

He left school at fifteen. They didn't want him anymore. The feeling was mutual, and he was glad and relieved to finally be rid of them, out of a system that had hemmed him in and left him with only one legacy to carry with him through life; That he was a loser…

That had been twelve years ago. Times had changed. The first meaningless jobs he had had were now only humorous memories, almost forgotten. The old box-guitar had been replaced a dozen times, although he still kept it as a fond souvenir. And the dark, oil-stained garage was only a memory of good times, now replaced by studios and concert halls. A far removal from his origins, but he would openly admit that it had been more fun there, in spite of the draught and the smell of the place.

He had gone his own way. Elvis and Lonnie were far from forgotten, but he had gradually developed his own style following his instincts and always looking for new ways to express his music, and always careful to stay away from the mainstream, where the competition was hardest and the likelihood of becoming just one of many faces was greatest. He had never wanted to follow the crowd, but preferred instead to go his own way.

Fame and fortune were nice to have, he would tell anyone who asked, but you had to work hard to achieve them. You also had to believe in yourself and what you were doing. He knew that better than most. It had been a long and hard road to travel, and had taken years of hard work and numerous disappointments, but he had enjoyed what he was doing and believed in it, and it had very slowly begun to give results, finally giving him the ultimate reward that others called stardom, but he called success.

Geoff had had more musical ability, but he had never had the faith, and had dropped out, preferring the safety of his father's newsagency to the uncertainty of making a living from the music they had made together. He had been disappointed, but understood all too well that on the road he was about to embark lay strewn the corpses of numerous others, more talented, more enthusiastic, and more determined, who had gone before him, and who had failed in the attempt. But he had to take the first step along that road and try to reach the end of it, still standing, or there would be no point to his life at all.

He had done it, Geoff had not. He had wanted him to, but Geoff had taken the straight road whereas he had chosen another for himself. That's life, Geoff would tell him whenever they met, but he was happy enough and success-ful enough in his own way, so didn't regret his decision "Except most of the time," he would ruefully tell him, only half joking.

They were sharing memories in the dressing room before the concert, re-laxed in each others company, enjoying themselves. They could hear the hus-tle and bustle going on outside as people prepared for the show, getting the lighting in place, the PA system directed to fill the venue, and all the greater or lesser details necessary for a successful performance for the three thousand fans who had bought their tickets weeks earlier, and could already now be heard arriving in the streets outside.

Although he had toured throughout the country and even abroad for many years, for some reason he had never before appeared in his home town. Now he was back for the first time as a performer, and he felt more excited at the prospect of his meeting with his own kind than he had thought he would. It would be fun, he thought, and looked forward to the start of the show.

The door opened and a head appeared through the opening. "There's some-one here to see you, Bobby," it said. He shrugged "And ... Who is it ...?" at the head. "He says he knows you from school," he said. He exchanged a curious look with Geoff, then nodded OK, and watched as a middle-aged man walked through the door with an uncertain smile on his face and his arm around the shoulders of a young girl.

"Hello, Robert," he said. "Do you remember me?"

As though he could ever forget! Mr. Burton had become older, but the forced bonhommie could not hide the mean lines of the face that had once tormented him on a daily basis.

Without waiting for a response, he moved the girl forward, as though us-ing her as a shield to ward off any unwanted words that might be aimed at him. "This is my youngest daughter, Janice," he told him. "She's a big fan." He paused as though this information was some kind of peace offering to appease him for past sins he had committed against him. "She wondered if she could have your autograph?" He held a book towards him. He ignored Geoff, who was sitting in the corner.

"Hello, Mr. Burton," he said slowly. "This is an unexpected surprise."

He took the book, and wrote in it.

Mr. Burton was obviously not at ease. "I've always been a big fan myself," he said through a fawning smile that could not quite hide his discomfort.

"That's nice …" He handed the book back, giving it to the girl. "Here you are, luv. Show it to your friends and make them jealous." He winked at her as he said it, and noticed her blush. "Did you know that your father and I are old acquaintances?" he asked, looking at her. "He used to thrash me whenever he got the chance."

Her father reacted uncomfortably. "Robert Joseph!" he said, a little too loudly. A little too sternly.

"Not Robert Joseph, Mr. Burton," he told him. "Bobby Joe!" He leaned back in his chair and stared at him. "Robert Joseph never existed," he said. "I was always Bobby Joe. You just never bothered to find out."

He got up and opened the door for them to leave. "By the way," he said, and nodded towards Geoff. "This is another of your earlier pupils," he told him. "You never said hello to him, so perhaps you would care to say goodbye," and he closed the door in his face.

"Good on you, Joe!" Geoff said. "He had that coming!"

He slapped him on the back. "Viva, Bobby Joe!"

"Nights are too long for me, because I'm losing you ..."
Losing You (Renard/Sigman)
Brenda Lee (1963)

Losing You

The moon was down. It was three o'clock in the morning and it could hardly be seen in the haze. The lights still glowing from the buildings around, mingled with the mist in a haunting melancholy of grey, while the lights from buildings farther away strained for attention through the mist that surrounded them. There was darkness all around, but when she looked up against the grey of the sky, the trees looming high above her stood out in black and sombre contrast, majestic and unmoving in the quiet of the night, sharing her thoughts in pragmatic silence.

She took a sip of wine and looked towards the sky to find the stars but they were blurred and hard to see. A disappointed twitch of the lips was all she allowed herself before she sipped a little more wine from the glass. She noticed a new darkness that had lowered itself upon the grey, drawing down upon it as she watched, and she wondered if it was bringing snow with it.

She heard the sound of a car accelerating in the distance. It was an angry sound. Aggressive. Hard. She heard it scream against the gears then relax as it eased into fourth, and purred away into the night.

She sighed and thought about the irritation and inconvenience if it should snow. The challenge of getting to work in the morning, and perhaps being stranded somewhere in the snow held little appeal, and she took a new sip from her glass as though to brace herself for the possibility. Time will tell, she thought, and breathed in the silence around her. Deeply. God, life was good, she told herself. In spite of everything.

The sex had not been good, but it had been there when she had wanted it. Although that had no longer been too often, it had still been there whenever she had felt the need. But now she only felt the peace and quiet around her, and was content in her own reverie. The mist around her seemed to erase all feelings that she might have had for the loss of the love she still felt for the man she had pushed way from her. Who had been faithful to her through all the years they had been together, and through all the times she had made him suffer in silence, watching as his pride and personality slipped away from him, yet knowing that he was impotent to save himself from her.

The feelings they had for each other had never changed, but their needs had, and with each altercation and slurred and unintended insult, the hurt had built up until it had reached a point from which there could be no return, although she knew that they both wished that there could be.

She gave a start as she suddenly realised that six months had now passed since that fateful night when he had begun to make love to her and she had savagely pushed him away from her. She grimaced as she remembered what she had said as he stared at her in shocked surprise and disappointment.

"You are disgusting and repulsive!" She had spat out the words with such venom and revulsion that she could not pretend that she had not meant them. The hurt that lit his face was hidden in the darkness of the bedroom but she could feel it. He had stared at her in silence for a long time, then had simply told her that if that was how she felt she need never again be afraid of being befouled by his touch. He would never again bother her with any kind of physical contact. Then he had turned on his side away from her, and neither of them had said another word through the night.

He had kept his promise. For six months they had pretended that her words were never said. For six months they had acted normally towards each other as though nothing had changed, although they both knew that it had. And for six months they had shared the same bed, back to back, without touching, and without sharing the thoughts that filled their minds and kept sleep at bay.

Because nothing was ever said, she never knew how deeply her words had wounded him. She knew that they had, but he never allowed her to see the scars that bled new blood every night as he waited for sleep with the words "You are disgusting and repulsive" repeating themselves in his mind, and taking up the same chorus again when he awoke in the mornings. Every night and every morning for six months, like a mantra repeating itself "You are disgusting and repulsive".

He had never been overconfident, accepting himself as being the average man that he was, and learning to live with it. Throughout the years they had been together he had felt happy and content sharing his life with the only woman he had ever loved, and considering her to be both beatiful and wonderful in every way. She had been the focus of his life for thirty years, and the changes in her through the years had only made her more appealing to him. He loved her, and she knew it. She also knew that she loved him too, but the changes that the years had made to him were not as favorable, and she had constantly chided him to lose weight, unaware of, and uninterested in the sacrifices this would entail for him. He had tried several times. Usually trying too hard in his attempts to mollify her, but the results were never in keeping with the investments, and he had remained the way he was; an average middle-aged man with a potbelly he couldn't lose.

Nonetheless he had been content with life and happy in his marriage. Until that night, when his whole world had crumbled, leaving him impotent and insecure with only her words to haunt him, and bitterness as a constant companion. And the pretence of normality to fill their empty existence.

He knew that he would never again be able to make love to her. To her, he was disgusting and repulsive, and he had therefore also become disgusting and repulsive in his own mind. As such he would never again be capable of believing that she, or any other woman, would want him. The little confidence he had once had, had been shattered by her words. He would never again be able to meet a woman's eyes without seeing the despise lurking behind them.

Her words had effectively castrated him. They had confirmed what he had always feared, but the shock of hearing them from the woman he loved and had shared his life with for thirty years, was like a dagger of truth visciously cutting away the false beliefs he had lived under, slashing and stabbing at his flesh until there was nothing left, and gauging his brain to let the false hopes and memories seep from it, to be filled by a void of disappointment and despair.

He knew he would never again be able to make love to her, but he also knew that he no longer wanted to. The pain she had caused him was too great. Her words had despised and destroyed him, leaving him with a sense of total betrayal and rejection that still clung to him like a leech, bleeding him of the remnants of self-respect that he had once had, and he knew he could never again look upon her with lust or desire. The very throught of her body against his, now only made him feel sick and angry. He felt miserably lonely and inadequate. Isolated and helpless …

Six months! she thought. God that is a long time …! She filled the glass with the remains of the bottle and replaced it on the veranda table. Still, the time had passed quickly and she had not really felt this period of celibacy as a burden. Sometimes perhaps, but not really. After all, the sex had not been good for the last years. It had become boring and stereotype. Just doing it to do it, with little enthusiasm and less satisfaction.

Thinking about it, she acceded the fact that he probably also felt the same way. But six months of celibacy was still a waste of a life. Two lives, she conceded. But this was after all nothing new for them, she thought. They had had others periods of celibacy and survived them. Thinking about them, she recalled that it had also then been her own reluctance that had kept them apart. Although then she had only rebuffed him, claiming lack of interest due to the change of life middle-aged women often went through.

But this time it was different. She knew she had brutally hurt him. The thought brought a guilty reaction that resulted in a new sip of wine, deeper than the others. But the feeling of guilt quickly passed.

There had been times when they had made love with passion and endurance for hours on end, repeatedly, again and again, from late night til morning, only resting in each others arms to build up new strength and desire. These exhausting and exhilarating bouts of lovemaking had mainly occurred when on holiday or on long weekends away from home, and they had lived on the memories for weeks afterwards, knowing that they had proved that they could, and would again, stimulate the passion that they both knew lived within them.

But holidays and long weekends always end, and the problems and routines of daily life are there to meet you at the airport when they are over. And with them the routine of work, the clock to follow, the bills to pay, and the half an hour under the blankets in the cold bedroom before sleep claims you to meet the appointment with the alarm clock early in the morning. Hardly an afrodisiac, she thought, and mumbled the pretension of a laugh.

No, sex was not important for her. She could live without it. She had other things to occupy her mind and her time, so she could manage without it. Her practical mind summarised the situation, and concluded with a "Who needs it, anyway?" in her mind. She felt a sudden tremble in her loins. It passed quickly, but she noticed it, and conceded with a smile that, o.k., perhaps once in a while.

As she stood on the veranda in the cool of the night with her thoughts roaming from the stars she could not see to the sex she did not miss, from the snow that might soon fall to the recall of the passion they had once shared but now had lost, he lay in bed still awake with only his thoughts for company, wishing for something more, and missing the warmth of a loving body next to him.

His needs were not extreme, but they were there. He wondered what life would have been with a warmer and more affectionate woman by his side. Someone less practical. Less cold and rejecting, than the woman he loved. Someone who would care for him for the man he was, instead of despising him for not being the man he was not.

He wondered if he was doomed to lifelong celibacy, or if someone, something, could bring back the feelings she had taken from him. Should he find a mistress? Or a prostitute? Someone who might bring back the belief in himself as a man? Someone who would pretend to love him for the money he paid them? Perhaps a more honest transaction than the farse she had made him live through all these years, he thought, then cast the thought from his mind. He knew he could not pretend, and he knew that he could not fuck for the sake of fucking. He needed more. Mutual love, respect and affection. What they had had in the early years, when she had still loved him.

Should he leave her? For what, he thought? He still loved her, and knew that he would always love her in spite of the way she held him from her and obviously despised him.

The thought suddenly crossed his mind; What if she leaves me? His heart skipped a beat. Could there be somebody else? Have I been that blind....? He turned over in the bed, facing the empty space beside him. I would kill her, he thought, but knew that he could never hurt her, and that it would probably kill him if it was true.

He thought about their friends. Were their marriages as perfect as they seemed, or were they too only living a lie? Pretending, like them?

Was he really disgusting and repulsive? He could not understand why. He accepted the fact that he was overweight, but no-one could call him fat or obese. Was he ugly? Did he smell? No, and no again. Just ordinary. Everyone could not be perfect. Perhaps she read too many women's magasines, he thought. In that case I must come out very unfavorably to all those models with their tight stomachs and three-day beards. But does that make me repulsive?

Although aware of all his shortcomings and failings, he could nonetheless not understand why she should despise him for being the man he was. He was the same man she had married. The same man who had fathered their children and raised them with her. The same man who had loved her and shown her affection for thirty years. A little heavier, and not as fit as he had once been, but still the same man. She knew that he loved her. She knew that he would do anything for her, and would do nothing to hurt her, yet she despised him.

Could that be the reason? That he loved her too much? Should he love her less and bring uncertainty to her? Would that help? He did not know, and there was no-one to ask, and no-one to tell him.

The glass was almost empty, and she had begun to feel the cold. Was he asleep? she wondered. Whatever … she decided, and came inside, locking the door to the veranda behind her. She turned off the lights and walked quietly into the bedroom, leaving the lights off as she entered.

He heard her undressing in the darkness, then felt the pressure on the mattress as she lowered herself to the bed. She felt him stir, and whispered: "Are you awake?"

"No," he said, and turned his back towards her.

Do you Remember, Do you Recall **1964**

- Harold Wilson became Prime Minister – Yes, but did it help?
- Gangling Cassius Clay put the voodoo on Sonny Liston to become World Champion
- The Beatles hit America and it was a k.o.'d in the first round
- A Hard Days Night showed the Fab 4 running and jumping up and down. Thank God they also found the time to play. (Wilfrid Brambell of Steptoe-fame played Wilfrid Brambell of Steptoe-fame in a way that nobody else could).
- Pirate Radio Caroline anchored off-shore and showed what the kids wanted to hear
- Sam Cooke was shot in a Los Angeles motel-room and left this Wonderful World
- The Dave Clark Five's Glad All Over toppled the Beatles from the nr.1 spot after they had held it for six weeks, and the press decided the Beatles were over the top (??)
- Michael Caine got his big break fighting Zulus with Stanley Baker
- Richard Burton played with Elizabeth Taylor in more ways than one in Cleopatra
- Sean Connery had an Odd-job getting the best of Goldfinger's handyman

Some popular records of the year that went right to the top:

- Glad All Over: The Dave Clark Five (Old Dave could really thump that drum …)
- Anyone Who Had A Heart couldn't help but love Cilla Black
- It's All Over Now: The Rolling Stones before they became circus clowns
- You Really Got Me: The Kinks with an intro that really made us sit up to listen
- Oh Pretty Woman: Roy Orbison the first time he introduced her to us
- I Feel Fine: The Beatles feeling good, and sounding it.

"And when I awoke I was alone, this bird had flown ..."
Norwegian Wood (Lennon/McCartney)
The Beatles "Rubber Soul" LP 1965

Norwegian Wood

"Big, isn't it?" The young man held his head high as he gazed up at the branches that seemed to reach to the sky.

His friend turned to him. "What?"

He didn't know if it was a question regarding his own statement, or if his friend was indicating that he had not heard him above the noise of the traffic and the crowd around them. He decided it must have been the first.

"The tree," he explained, and nodded towards the pine.

"Yes ...", his friend acknowledged with little enthusiasm, then returned his attention to the crowd around them. He thought for a moment, then absent-mindedly added "Lot of wood."

"What?" It was difficult to hear above the noise, but their minds were not on conversation so they weren't really listening anyway.

He turned to his friend to make sure he had heard him. "The tree." He pointed towards it. "There's a lot of wood in the tree."

His friend mouthed a silent uninterested "Oh" of understanding, then re-turned his gaze to the giant Christmas tree. After a few moments alone with his thoughts, he added "It's from Norway," he said. "Norwegian wood."

New moments of silent reflection.

"They've got big woods over there."

"What?"

He raised his voice, and tried again. "In Norway," he shouted. "They've got big woods over there."

His friend shrugged a "So what?" then returned to his own thoughts. After a few moments of silence he corrected him. "Big woods are forests".

"What?"

"When a wood is big, they call it a forest," he explained. "A big wood is a forest."

The other man considered this. "Still a lot of wood", he insisted.

His friend wasn't listening. "Would what?" he asked.

"What?" His friend didn't understand.

"What would?"

"The wood in Norway. The Norwegian wood", he explained.

"Oh..." Not interested.

They were standing in the crowd in Trafalgar Square waiting for the Christmas lights to be turned on to light the huge pine tree before them. It was chilly, and they would normally have preferred the warmth of a pub, but they knew from earlier experience that there would be many attractive girls in the crowd, and that the communal feeling of Christmas Coming made it easier to make contact, and the possibility of getting a girl interested made the chill of the evening acceptable.

Their eyes roamed the crowd, sometimes resting on a face or a pair of legs, before continuing the search, like hungry sharks in murky water looking for the perfect prey.

"Hey," he nudged his friend. "Look at them," he said, and nodded his head towards two young blondes who had just joined the crowd.

His friend gave a low whistle in agreement, and they both began to move through the crowd with their eyes held steady on the unwitting focus of their attention, as they circled in the prey like lions preparing for the chase.

They sidled up behind them, and allowed themselves to be jostled by the crowd so they were pushed against them. "Sorry, darling," they excused themselves in unison, as they steadied themselves against the girls, holding on to an arm for balance. They smiled apologies at the faces that had turned towards them. The girls smiled back, then returned their attention to the tree. "They're beauties," they thought as they saw them close, then turned on whatever charm they had in an attempt to make a conquest.

"It's big isn't it?" one said to the back of their heads, and nodded towards the tree as they turned towards him.

"Yes, it is," they answered, then looked at each other and smiled, recognising a come-on when it came.

"It's from Norway," his friend informed them.

"Yes, I know", one of the girls replied, smiling. Then added, "So am I."

"What?" they echoed, not hearing what she had said.

"I am too," she told them.

They still didn't hear her, and exchanged blank looks hoping for enlightenment without finding it. Having nothing else to offer they only said "Oh."

One of them decided that he couldn't let this hang in the air unattended, so he asked her. "What are you, too?"

She wasn't listening. "Who?" she asked back, bending her ear to his mouth to hear him.

The noise from the crowd, and the Christmas music being piped through the speakers made conversation difficult.

"What?" He was becoming bewildered.

His friend saved him. "She asked you, who?" he told him.

"You what?" the noise of the crowd didn't help his confusion.

"Who!" his friend increased the volume of his voice. "Who! Not what!"

"Who, what!???" He was now totally confused. The expression on his face showed it clearly.

They noticed the girls. They had both turned towards them, and were now laughing uncontrollably at his confusion, holding each other by the arm for support. The boys became even more bewildered, but then relaxed as they understood the absurdity of the situation, and joined in the laughter, thus bonding in a way that they could never have contrived to do.

They stayed in the crowd until the lights were lit, then moved to a nearby pub for a drink. They were all obviously enjoying themselves, and the two young men felt that they might get lucky. They moved from one pub to another, and finally found themselves in the basement of a rock club in Soho, where they drank and danced and exchanged the first kisses.

They were feeling good when they came into the clear night air as the club closed, and the suggestion of continuing the night at a party the girls knew of, was welcomed with exhuberant expectation.

It was a new basement location. They walked through the people standing by the open door, and into the noise inside the flat. There was little furniture. Instead there were dozens of cushions strewn about the floor were people sat or lay about, some in groups, others alone, and one or two couples in passionate embraces, unembarrassed by the people around them.

"Get a beer from over there," one of the girls pointed, "and bring one for us too." They had by now all got to the stage where the evening's alcohol intake was making its mark, and loosening their inhibitions. The kisses had become more passionate and the closeness of their bodies more intimate. They found a space on the floor, and allowed their desire to explore and experience, and they felt the excitement mounting.

"Want a blow?" He turned his head to see a girl kneeling above him, and his blank face showed a dozen questions racing through his mind as he wondered what she meant. Then he saw the rolled cigarette she was offering him, loosely packed and ready to be lit. He looked at her face, then thought, "Why not?" and took it. "Got one more?" he asked, and got one.

He rested his back against the wall and lit up, taking a deep drag, filling his lungs to the maximum, then slowly exhaled, enjoying the experience. He took another drag, then offered the joint to the girl by his side. She declined. "One more for me then," he thought, remembering the one he had in his pocket. He kissed her, then took another drag as he began to feel the warmth creeping into his mind and body. He took a swig of beer, then another drag, and felt relaxed and content, and smiled at the young blonde by his side.

Later in the night, they found a small unused bedroom, and were soon lying naked on the mattress there. The last he could remember was how beautiful she was, and how dizzy he had become. He fell asleep with a whimsical, content expression on his face and a stiff erection to share his slumber.

He woke up in the morning with only a searing hangover for company. The girl was gone, and so was his erection. He found a few remnants of the party still lying around in various stages of sleep, but his friend and the blonde girls they had been with, were all gone. "Bloody idiot," he scolded himself miserably. "Too much booze and too many joints ..." He remembered it all too well. She had been naked in his arms, and he had fallen asleep. God, how embarrassing! And now she was gone. But his parched throat and throbbing head claimed his total attention, and the embarrassment of the night was placed on hold in the back of his mind as he gathered his clothes and put them on, wet his dry throat with the last drops from a bottle he found in a corner, and climbed the steps to the pavement, to go home, alone.

The two friends met in the local pub in the evening.

"What the hell happened to you?" his friend asked, perplexed.

He looked at him. "What do you mean?" He knew what he meant, but wanted to forget it all.

"We were doing great, then your bird came storming out from the bedroom, and they both just packed up and left." His friend was still in frustrated shock, disappointed and angry.

He frowned as the memories came back to him; her blonde hair in his face and her naked body warm against his. And his own stupidity.

His friend continued. "I was doing allright until she came out", he said. "Whatever it was you were doing in that bedroom really cocked things up for me," he told him accusingly. He noticed the misery in the other man's face, and allowed his irritation to subside, suddenly feeling sympathy for him. He took a sip of his beer, then grudgingly admitted, "Ah, well," he said resignedly, "she probably wouldn't have gone all the way, anyway," and he shrugged.

His friend turned his face from him to stare disconsolately into his beer. He sighed deeply, took a mouthful, and sadly said to himself, "But the Norwegian would".

"The only man who could ever reach me,
was the son of a preacher man …"
Son of a Preacher Man (Hurley/Wilkins)
Dusty Springfield 1968

Son of a Preacher Man

Jenny Duncan thought life was passing her by. She was twenty-seven and had still not had a serious relationship. Some of her friends were married, and others would be taking the plunge in the next year or so, whereas she was still single with no immediate prospects of finding a candidate to share her life with.

She was no vestal virgin, but had had her flings with young men she had met at dances or parties, enjoying their company as long as it lasted, which was usually not for more than a date or two. Some of her conquests had shown interest in developing the relationship, but she had always found some reason to smother it and let the flame die out before it had a chance to properly ignite.

In her eyes, the men she met were never quite good enough. There was always something lacking, something to hold her back. She wanted perfection, and realised that she would probably never find it, but nonetheless used such a demand as an excuse to withdraw from further involvement. She sometimes wondered if making such impossible demands, was really subconsciously a way of avoiding the responsibility of giving herself to another, and thus the possibility of rejection and pain. Love couldn't hurt her if she held it at bay. Without emotion there could be no emotional involvement. So she sought perfection from an emotional distance that allowed her the freedom to pull away before feeling the desire to stay.

Some of her encounters had swayed her, tempting her to know them better and allowing them to know her, but she had resisted the temptation and floundered back to dry land from where she could safely resume her independence, unchecked by the waves of desire that might have drawn her under the water to drown in its embrace.

After such encounters it would take time before she again dared to approach the water's edge and let the ripples of temptation lap at her feet, even as she prepared to run from them.

She wanted love. She wanted a relationship that would last. She wanted someone to share her life with. But she was not prepared to open her heart to let them in. That would only make her vulnerable, and she feared rejection and what it could do to her, more than she desired them. By not allowing herself to become vulnerable, she was keeping herself safe from rejection. By not allowing love to come into her life, love could never hurt her. So love was something she desperately wanted but was not prepared to give, to get.

The fact that she had only had short affairs through the years, meant that there were a number of men who had known her. Many of these had also known her sexually. She would sometimes feel ashamed when she thought about them, knowing that there were too many, and that the sum of her affairs may have given her a reputation that she felt she didn't deserve.

Sometimes she felt that the interest shown towards her by new male acquaintances was based on the reputation she feared that she might have, and that their interest was in her availability and in the knowledge that she did not want involvement. A good basis for an easy lay for any red-blooded young man on the make.

The very thought could make her distraught. She knew that she was not promiscuous, but counting up the number of affairs she had had through the years would make her seem to be. Had she had a few steady boyfriends with relationships that had each lasted for some time, there would have been no reason to question her morals. The fact that her relationships had never lasted long did not make her promiscuous, but in many's eyes, the fact that there had been many such relationships through the years, did.

She was twenty-seven and had been a bridemaid twice. This would be the third time. Three times the bridemaid, never the bride, she thought. She was turning into an old maid while all her friends were getting married. She wondered what was wrong with her, but knew the answer before the question was finished - she was too afraid of failure and too frightened of involvement to let any man get close enough to learn to love her. And she couldn't help it. Some kind of barrier prevented her from crossing the divide from desire to fulfillment. From wishing for love to getting and giving it. Holding her back from trying to find it. Gripping her with the fear of failure.

The wedding was a lively affair. Her friend had been excited and nervous and had taken a valium to control the one and two healthy gins to control the other, with the obvious results. Walking down the aisle is never easy, but with that particular combination inside her head, and a bridal gown that had to be balanced as she walked, it took determination and concentration to make it. Walking behind her, Jenny Duncan, three-times bridemaid though she was, was relieved when she finally did.

The groom had had his own particular problems, arriving late after having been taken to the hospital with stomach pains. The best man had had to support him to the altar, while the guests sitting in their pews frowned their disapproval, taking his pale features and stumbling approach, for too much drink. The best man had to support him throughout the ceremony, and had immediately driven him back to the hospital when it was over, leaving the guests guessing and the bride to cut the cake on her own.

The bride was in tears. Her wedding was spoiled, her reception would have to be held without the groom, and her wedding night would be spent on her own. She was miserably hysterical, and Jenny Duncan could only try to console her as best she could, and under the circumstances, her best could never be good enough.

"Excuse me." She turned her head and saw a young man showing genuine concern for them. It showed clearly in his face. "Is there anything I can do to help?" he asked. She had noticed him in the church. He had handed out the hymn books to the guests, and she recalled that he had been standing to the side during the ceremony.

"No, it's allright," she told him, as she held her arms around her friend and felt her tears.

She expected him to leave them alone, but he didn't move. "Let's bring her in here," he suggested, and gently moved them through a door. He pulled a chair towards them. "Please sit down," he said to the distraught bride. "You'll feel better." He took her by the arm and lowered her into the chair, then glanced at Jenny Duncan. "I'll get a glass of water for her," he told her, then left the room.

Although the drama of the wedding ceremony still dominated the function, the reception had become quite lively, possibly because the drama that the guests had experienced earlier had enhanced their thirst, and, as they quenched it, the voices became louder, the laughter that had been with-held for so long while sharing the misery of the bride, was now heard more often and louder, and the dancing became wilder as inhibitions were laid to rest.

The bride had gradually regained her strength and joined the reception, and partaken of its pleasures, not in the way she had expected to, but gradually falling into a fatalistic acceptance of what had happened, that allowed her to enjoy the evening in spite of everything.

Jenny Duncan had found a chair by the wall. She was sitting alone with her thoughts, thinking about the events of the day as she stared into the glass she held in her hand, feeling compassion for her friend and the terrible disappointment the day had held for her. She noticed someone in the process of sitting down on a seat to her side, and casually glanced up to see that it was the young man who had helped them earlier in the day. He glanced back at her, and smiled shyly. "Hello," he said, then turned his gaze into the room.

She smiled back. "Hello," she answered non-commitedly, then joined his gaze at the general activity in the room, as she allowed her earlier thoughts to return to her mind.

They sat in silence for a few moments, and she noticed that he seemed nervous, as though trying to make a decision but not knowing how to do it. He turned towards her and gave her a smile, then turned away again. After a few moments he shook his head and said "Poor girl," and sighed.

She turned her head towards him. "Yes," she agreed. "On her own on her wedding day. It's really terrible for her …"

He lost interest in the room and turned towards her. "Would you like something to drink?" he asked her. She shook her head and indicated the half-full glass in her hand. He got up and moved to the chair next to her with a "Do you mind …?" She shrugged and shook her head again. "My name's Derek," he told her, and shook her hand, introducing himself. He nodded across the room towards the vicar standing in a corner with a glass in his hand and in jovial conversation with a group of guests. "That's my father," he told her. "The vicar." She looked across at him with mild interest, then back to the man by her side.

"Is that why you were at the church?" she asked him. "I thought you were one of the family or something." She thought for a moment, then asked "Do you always help out at weddings?"

"Only when I'm at home," he replied. "I'm at university," he informed her. "Theology." He laughed. "I'm going into the family business," he said, and smiled.

She thought it was a pleasant laugh. And a nice smile.

They talked, and she found it easy to talk with him. She found herself enjoying his company. He was nice to be with, and surprisingly funny once he had begun to feel comfortable in her presence, and she soon found herself laughing or chuckling as they talked. She relaxed as she saw him relaxing, and the more at ease she felt, the more she opened herself to him. They danced and it seemed natural to be in his arms, and she gradually began to feel a warmth for him, and found herself smiling more often than she was used to, and the smiles clung to her longer than they would normally have done.

He took her home when the reception was over, and they lingered for some time outside her door, talking quietly, as though neither wanted the evening to end. They had finally parted with a gentle good-night kiss. There had been no passion in it, and no attempt to get closer. It had just been a nice and natural way to end the evening, and they smiled fondly at each other as she opened the door and went inside.

She hummed a tune to herself as she undressed and climbed into bed, where she found little sleep to keep her company through the night. When she awoke in the morning, she awoke with the memory of him in her thoughts, and she smiled contentedly thinking of him. As the day passed by, she found that she couldn't erase him from her mind, and further, she didn't want to. She wanted him there, and she already missed him. She acknowledged that he was not particularly handsome. But she did think that he was attractive. He would never be the life and soul of any party. But she thought he was fun to be with. Nobody would call him exciting. But she found him to be interesting.

Had she been disappointed when he had been content with one tender kiss? She thought about it before deciding that she had found it to be surprisingly refreshing not to have to ward off someone who felt it to be his masculine obligation and right to try to score a century in the first innings. Disappointing? No, on the contrary. It had been natural and nice.

She wondered if she had fallen in love, but laughed at the suggestion, then conceded that she liked him a lot. But love …? Nobody falls in love in one day! Do they …?

He had promised to call her, and she waited by the telephone wanting it to ring. But the days passed with no call. She couldn't get him out of her mind, and the more days that passed without the call she was praying for, the more he dominated her thoughts.

She couldn't believe it. She had always had control of her feelings, and now she was like a lost child unable to find her way, completely infatuated by a man she had only spent a few hours with, wanting nothing more than to be with him again, and desperate for him to call her, to hear his voice again. She wanted him. She had been used to turning away men who wanted her. To controlling the relationship, deciding when to end it, and doing so when she felt that she might be losing control of her feelings, and becoming dependent on someone. Now, she found herself out of control, wanting the relationship to work and needing him. The only man she had ever really wanted. And she hardly knew him …

She laughed at herself. A vicar's son …! A preacher in a dog-collar in the C of E…! And I'm praying that he's going to call me …! Then the laughter stopped and she became silent. What if he didn't call? What if he didn't want to see her again? The very thought brought concern to her face, and she became gloomy and worried. Please call, she thought. Please call …

The call came unexpectedly as she was lying in the bath, and she almost slipped as she rushed across the tiles and into the hall as naked as the day she was born, dripping suds and water on the carpet as she grabbed the telephone and pressed it to her ear, Please, please, please! screaming in her mind.

She almost sagged with relief as she heard his voice.

"Jenny," he said. "I've really missed you." She felt her heart skip a beat. "I've been thinking about you all week, but I've been afraid to call you." Another skipped beat. "I don't know if you want to, but it would be lovely if we could go out together tonight." She sighed audibly. "But only if you're free," he said with concern straining in his voice.

She sighed deeply, and the smile was for herself. "Yes, please," she said.

"Yes, please…"

Do you Remember, Do you Recall **1965**

- Winston Churchill died to national mourning
- Mary Quant, the mini-skirt, Carnaby Street, London was the centre of world fashion
- The Beatles were awarded MBE's, much to the consternation of the establishment
- Anthony Quinn became Zorba the Greek and taught Alan Bates to dance
- Rex Harrison taught Audrey Hepburn her vowels in My Fair Lady
- Julie Andrews was Mary Poppins. Supercalafragalistic … How did it go anyway?

Some popular records that went right to the top:
- Satisfaction: The Rolling Stones the way they were supposed to be
- I Got You Babe: Sonny and Cher in sheep-skins
- Tears: Ken Dodd without his tickle-stick
- The Carnival Is Over: The Seekers, with Judith Durham's fantastic voice
- Mr. Tambourine Man: The Byrds with a new sound that made Dylan sound good
- Help!: The Beatles still on top without any help from their friends.

"I smoke old stogies I have found ..."
King of the Road (Miller)
Roger Miller (1965)

King of the Road

"You've got to have pride, son. Without it, you're nothing." The old tramp looked at the younger man as they rested on the sunbaked ground with their backs against an old oak tree. "Don't never let nobody call you a tramp," he went on, and raised his chin defiantly as he spoke. "You're a traveller, not a tramp!"

He broke a blade of grass from the ground, and placed it in his mouth, then chewed on it thoughtfully, as he gazed towards the sky. "You see son, a tramp does this from necessity. Because he has to." He shrugged. "Got no other choice, you see." The touch of a smile crossed his face. "Now a traveller, like me, he does it for choice, because he wants to."

He turned his head towards the other man. "For the freedom it gives him, and because it's the life he's chosen to lead." He paused for a moment, thinking. "A tramp hasn't got no pride, you see," he continued. "If you've got no pride, you're just a tramp, and nobody respects you." He shook his head sadly, then turned his gaze back to the sky, and continued, "But if you're a traveller, like me, you've got your pride," he said, then pointed to his chest. "I'm a traveller," he said. "Always have been since the war, and always will be. And proud of it!" He nodded his head twice as if to confirm his statement.

They were in the lower regions of the western Pennines and had joined forces after meeting earlier in the day and finding that they both were heading in the general direction of North Wales. The younger man was in his thirties. The fact that the older man adressed him as "son" had nothing to do with either age or family ties, (although when truth be told, he never could be sure of the latter with the life he had led). However unintended, it was a way of showing his superiority, like a dog pissing high on the trunk of a tree to put competition in its place.

The old tramp fumbled in the folds of his coat and eventually brought out a small tin of tobacco. He opened it and found a cigarette stub among the strands of loose tobacco. He took it out and studied it as though it was a fine Havana cigar to be savoured in anticipation before enjoying it, then he found a match and lit it. He replaced the used match in the tin, and pressed the lid shut. He took a deep swallow, and closed his eyes in contentment as he slowly exhaled the smoke to let it ease from his lips in a thin stream.

"This is the life," he sighed contentedly. "This is the life …"

The other man had often heard of him before meeting him by chance that day. He knew that he had been on the road for most of his life, and that he was an experienced traveller. The best of them all, they said. They called him the King. The King of the Road. He knew everybody - at least, he knew the people who mattered for a traveller; the farmers, the villagers of the countryside, the local policemen and the wardens and vicars of the small country churches, and of course, the people working the fairs that travelled through the country with their merry-go-rounds and sideshows. He knew them all. And they knew him. Or of him.

Other travellers would enquire about him whenever they met on the road, and would exchange stories they had heard about him. Nothing exciting, but nonetheless, the myths that had grown through the years, had made him interesting enough to be the object of their discussions, and in the loneliness of life on the road, anything was worth talking about once they had found someone to listen.

The myths were of course heavily coloured by rumour, and with each rumour the myth of the man grew, while he himself travelled in content ignorance, unaware of what others said about him. Some claimed to know that he had been in prison for some devious crime, while others were certain that he was wanted by the police and travelling to keep from them. Others again claimed to have heard that he had come from a wealthy family that had disowned him, and that he had taken to the road in shame. There were all kinds of stories, but they were only told when two travellers met. They would then be carried with them to their next meeting, when they would be enhanced by imagination and the need for entertainment, as they spent the night in some lonely spot in the woods.

There was however little truth to the tales that were told about him. Yes, he had spent nights in police stations, but usually at his own request to have a dry place to sleep for the night, and the country bobbies were normally quite understanding when he came to their door. Once he had had to spent a night in a cell at the police's insistence rather than his own, after there had been a burglary in a village that he had happened to be passing through. However, the misunderstanding was quickly cleared up, and he could leave again the next day with a clear conscience and a full belly after enjoying a hearty breakfast, and a good night's sleep.

He had never been a criminal. Whatever he accumulated on his travels, he got from his charm and his wit, both of which endeared him to whoever he might happen to meet, man or woman. But most of all the children. He had known from the beginning that he would always win the parents if he won the kids, but he had never used this knowledge intentionally. He simply had a natural empathy for children that brought them close to him, and he enjoyed talking with them. And, of course, being a traveller, he had all the time in the world for them. As he approached a village or a farm, walking with his characteristic limp, the older children would recognise him and call out "It's old uncle John, the tramp," and welcome him with questions of his travels since his last appearance. Younger children who had never seen him before, would be more wary, and call out to their parents "There's a tramp coming!" But that was before they came under his magical spell, and he also became uncle John the tramp, for them.

A psychologist would probably have defined the obvious enjoyment he showed when among children, as some kind of compensation for the loss he had experienced during the war. He had been too old to be in the army, but he did have a job, a home and a family. It was a direct hit. He was out. His family was not. His wife and their three children had been at home when the bomb fell. He was not.

He was left alone and destitute with only the clothes he wore on his back. After the funeral, he had walked away, kept walking, and never gone back.

That had been twentytwo years ago, but he still kept walking.

Everyone had heard the myths and the rumours, but nobody knew the truth, because he had never told it. Not to anyone. And he never would. Instead he had silently carried it with him through all these years, yet never allowing it to cloud his smile or to lose the open charm he always carried with it.

"Where're you heading for?" The question showed only mild interest, as though it was just to make conversation.

The old man scratched his chin as he stretched the muscles in his face into a grimace. "I don't know," he replied. "Reckon I might go to Rhyl," he said, "Get some sea air, and make a couple of bob at the fair." He yawned, and stretched his arms. "Might stop in Wrexham for the market. I'll see when I get there."

This was the way he had lived his life since the war, and it had become natural for him. Going nowhere at his leisure when he wanted to. Then somewhere else when it suited him. And then back again, as he pleased. With only his thoughts to keep him company, and a knapsack on his back.

"You know what?" he asked into the air. "I sometimes feel sorry for all the people I meet on my travels." He folded his hands behind his neck, and adjusted his head to be more comfortable. "They've got all they need, but they still want more. All the time, more." His mouth curved down at the thought. "More, more, more." He turned his head slightly to look at the other tramp. "Don't they know that they're only building their own prisons?"

As the chain of thoughts came to him, his voice became more persuasive. "I mean, the more you own, the more you're stuck, aren't you? You can't leave it all behind, and you've got to work to pay for the flaming things, haven't you!?" He shook his head at the thought. "They've got no lives," he said. "They're only existing. Existing just to pay for what they don't need. And buying what they don't need keeps them stuck. Imprisoned!"

The other man nodded his agreement, while the old tramp considered what he had just said, then decided that what he had just said, made sense, and he too nodded in agreement, satisfied with his own words and their conclusion.

They sat in silence for a few minutes, neither of them feeling the need to speak.

"I'm not." The old man broke the silence.

The other tramp turned his head with a question on his face. "You what?" he asked.

The old man looked at him. "What?"

"You're not what?" he asked, wondering what they were talking about.

The old man relaxed again as he understood the misunderstanding. "Existing," he explained. "I'm not just existing."

He absentmindedly moved his hand through the air with the palm up as though to indicate the world around them. "Not like them," he said. He thought about it. "No. I'm free, see? I do what I like, when I like, and there's nobody to tell me different." He looked up to the branches of the tree above him. "Free as a bird I am. Free as a bird…"

Their ways parted a few miles later as the country lane came to a junction. "I think I'll go this way," the old tramp said, with no apparent reason to explain his choice. The other tramp decided to take the other road, so they parted. "See you around," they both said, as they walked away.

The old tramp watched for a moment as the younger man moved away, "Stay proud, son," he called after him. "Stay proud!" Then he hitched his knapsack on his shoulder and wandered on.

"We gotta get out of this place, if it's the last thing we ever do ..."
We Gotta Get Out of This Place (Mann/Weil)
The Animals 1965

We Gotta Get Out of this Place

Light clouds shifted gently across the blue of the sky as far as he could see. It was good weather for a long drive, and he was enjoying himself, feeling the freedom as the miles passed by him. The traffic isn't bad, he thought. I've seen it a lot worse. Driving on the motorway alone with your thoughts, isn't a bad way of spending a few hours. You get a chance to think. To relax. To be alone. He checked the mirror then accelerated past a column of trailers grinding their way up the left lane, smiling to himself with the pleasure of feeling the horsepower pressing him back against the seat as he pushed in the accelerator.

He hummed a tune, then bent towards the dashboard and pressed the button for the radio, and leaned back as the music came from the speakers. *When the going gets tough the tough get going* … He sang with the song, tapping his fingers to the beat on the steering wheel. Billy Ocean. Great! He was good, he thought, and kept tapping the beat. Not like the Animals, but still good. What the hell happened to them, anyway? He had read somewhere that Eric Burdon was in Los Angeles apparently living high on booze and dope, but still making music like in the old days at the Club A Go Go. And he knew that Alan Price still did the odd show. Wasn't Chad still in the business down in London somewhere? Producing records or something? But what the hell happened to the Animals?

He joined in the chorus again, singing with determined gusto, and not caring if he didn't hit the high notes. There was nobody there to hear him anyway.

His mind blanked for a few moments, before it began to function again. I bet they all miss the Go Go. I bet they'd all want to be back there just one more time, he thought. Just for fun and for the memories. Instead they all Went Went, he said aloud, and chuckled at the bad joke.

He stared at the motorway before him without thinking of anything in particular, then said quietly, "Like I did …", and the memories began to roll through his mind in chapters, a little here, and a little there, but all from the hopelessness of the Newcastle he had left twenty years earlier.

He closed the door behind him and began to walk along the pavement. It was still dark and the lights from the lampposts cast shadows across the street. He pulled up the collar of his jacket against the cold. He noticed the door opening three houses down, at nr. 17, then heard it close as another shadow joined him, walking by his side, almost in step, both looking down at the pavement as they moved. "Morning Harry," he said. "Hello Jim," his companion mumbled in reply, without looking up.

It had always been like that, even when they had been kids going off to school together; "Morning Harry." "Hello Jim." Then walking together to wherever they were going. To school, or, as they had now been doing for the past ten years, to work. They had grown up together as neighbours and friends, and had remained both throughout their lives.

They rounded the corner at the end of the street and saw the lights from the factory a stone's throw away. They approached it in silence, and only spoke again when they went inside one of the buildings, one moving to the left, the other to the right.

"See you later," Jim said without looking at him. "Yea". They went to their respective work areas and found their machines waiting for them just as they had left them only hours earlier. Another new day had begun, just like every other.

He had hated that bloody factory. He had hated the machine. And he had hated everything about the bloody job there. God, I'm lucky, he thought. I could still be there …

He turned down the volume of the car radio. The music they were playing was distracting him from his thoughts, and he was suddenly interested in what was happening in his mind and didn't want it disturbed.

I haven't done too badly, he thought. Could be worse. He frowned and nodded his head in acknowledgement of the fact. A lot bloody worse! It had been hard to start with. Three jobs. God love us, he shook his head. Three jobs! How did I do it? Getting through it all with three or four hours sleep? That had been hard to get used to, but now he couldn't manage to sleep longer if he had tried. It had got in the blood. But hard? Yes, he admitted, it had been bloody hard! Then a grin of satisfaction crossed his face, as he felt the pride of achievement worming its way into his head.

Looking back though, I suppose it wasn't that bad. It was hard, but I was young and tough, and I could take it. Without being aware of it, he began to mumble *When the going gets tough the tough get going,* once again, although Billy Ocean had left the airwaves miles before.

He had worked at the hotel from early morning, then at a pub in the afternoons, and finally the bar at the club. It hadn't been difficult to find work in London, and the possibilities that had suddenly opened themselves to him there, had made him want to take every damn job he could find! They weren't fancy jobs, but they paid a wage, and with him working all the time, he had never had a chance to spend the stuff. It had been a hard life, but it had been worth it, he thought, and smiled. But us Geordies can take it, he thought, and meant it.

Newcastle had been the slagheap of England when he had lived there. A dogshit on the pavement that nobody had taken the time to clear away, and everyone else avoided. A wart on the conscience of Harold bloody Wilson and all the rest of them. They had all always voted Labour in the hope that they would help, but they never gave a damn. Except at the elections. And neither did anyone else. Nobody was interested. Nobody cared. It was too far from London, and too far gone to save.

He had lived in the slums lurking along the banks of the Tyne, in a street of terraced houses that had been built in the previous century. They weren't pretty and they weren't warm, but that was all they had, and was where he came from. That was his home. There, lives were as distant from those of the people living in the suburbs of the city, as was possible. What they called home, the others wouldn't have allowed their dogs to live in. The highlight of the year for them might be a day trip to the beach to wade in the chill and murky North Sea waves of Whitley Bay, just to get some air.

But people there had shared hard times before, and had somehow got through them. His father had often mentioned the Jarrow march to London, and had told him the reasons for it. His grandfather had actually been a part of it, resolutely walking all the way with the other men who had demanded justice for themselves and their families. Who had demanded jobs. Who had demanded food. And who had got nothing but promises. They had known how hard life could be, and it had shown on them after years of living with it, but they had still been there when he had left, with their pride still intact although fate had taken everything else from them.

They had eaten their dinners in the downstairs room and slept in the draughty bedroom upstairs, but their real home had been the pub on the corner where they could find some warmth and company in order to forget the miserable lives they led. A pint of ale whenever they could afford it was the reward for suffering the lives they led, and was often all it took to take their minds from it. At least, for a while.

They had had their football and their pride. Basically two sides of the same coin. But little else.

He saw the lights of a police car flashing ahead and slowed his speed as he passed an accident. Poor sods, he thought. Hope nobody's hurt, then accelerated again as he passed them.

He had put his hard earned money to good use. It had come as a surprise to him when he had seen what he had saved after seven years in the Smoke. He had never dreamed that he would ever have that much. He had first been proud, then worried that he might lose it, then excited as he thought what he could do with it. But he had been patient and had kept working the three jobs for another five years, watching it grow while he had considered his options.

He had eventually put it all into a pub on the outskirts of London. A pub with a menu. A pub with a bit of class. It had shown a profit from the first day, and now he owned two. And a bungalow with a nice garden, he reminded himself.

He preferred wine now, but admitted that he still enjoyed a Newcastle Brown whenever he could get one, and he suddenly looked forward to tasting one when he got home.

Home? I live in London now, he thought, wondering why he had said it. My home is in London for God's sake! He allowed the thought to relax itself, then admitted that he still missed the old place that had once been his home. As long as I don't have to stay there, he thought, and chuckled to himself. As long as I don't have to stay....

"We've got to get out of this place, before it's too bloody late! Before it smothers us, and we become like them." Harry had nodded his head towards three older men who were huddled in a corner talking, holding their glasses as though they were afraid to let them go. They were only in their early fifties but looked twenty years older. They wore worn jackets. Their shirts were collarless, with scarves to hold the chill from the throat. Their faces were ashen grey, with stubble showing, and they all needed a haircut that they could obviously not afford. Only one had his own teeth. The second had a set that didn't fit and moved in his mouth as he spoke. The third had none. Only his gums.

He had sighed. "Ay," he said quietly, and turned his head back to the table, and studied his glass in silence.

Harry wasn't finished. "Look," he said, "I'm effing twentysix and still living with me mam in the back bedroom! I've got no money, no prospects, and in twenty years I'm going to be just like them fellers over there!"

He raised his glass to his lips, but stopped before it reached them. "The factory pays me a pittance," he continued. "After I've paid for my keep, I've got just enough left to get drunk trying to get a bird at the dance on Saturday night, and a pint or two during the week, and that's it!" Harry took a sip of beer. "And do you know what?" He paused for a moment. "Every bloody day, I thank my lucky stars that I've still got that bloody job, because there are no others around here if I lose it. Then where would I be!?" He stared into his friend's face. "Eh?" he asked. "You tell me. Where would I be then?"

Jim had heard it all before. Often. He understood his friend's frustration and shared it. However, in contrast to Harry, he did not want to leave the environment in which he had been raised. It wasn't much, he freely admitted, but at least he knew what he had, and the only people he knew or cared about were there, and they were all in the same situation, together.

How many times had Harry said it? he wondered. Every damned week for years. Especially when he had had a pint or two and was feeling especially despondent. Harry had desperately wanted to leave for years, and wanted him to leave with him. To find a new and better life. He had been willing to go anywhere, sometimes even mentioning Canada and Australia. Perhaps he had been right, he thought. They say people live good lives in those places. But anywhere would have been better than the hopelessness of dirty old Newcastle.

After years of bullying him, badgering him and pleading with him, Harry had finally worn him down and Jim had unenthusiastically succombed to Harry's relentless bombardments, and agreed to go with him to London in search of better prospects and a little hope.

He remembered how Harry's face had lit up when he had eventually agreed, as though a weight had been lifted from his shoulders, and he had suddenly become alive again like a zombie who had been given a brain and something to live for.

He leant forward to look up at the sky. It was becoming darker, and it had begun to drizzle. He could see heavier clouds ahead. Typical, he thought, and leaned back against the seat. The sun never shines on the Tyne …. he sighed. Or perhaps it just seems that way. He would soon be approaching the south side of the river, and began to take more notice of the signs making sure that he would take the right turn-off.

Yes, Harry had become a different man after he had finally got him to agree to go with him. They had made their plans, and suddenly they also had dreams and schemes to bring them through the days. Where there before had been nothing to believe in, there was now suddenly no limit to their possibilities, and they had become more and more enthusiastic as the time for their departure slowly approached. Although Harry's enthusiasm infected Jim, he was still uncertain about the whole project, and would willingly have backed down if Harry had shown any sign of second thoughts. But Harry's enthusiasm had remained high throughout.

It was raining now, and he turned on the wipers, as he moved off the motorway. A thought struck him, and he opened the window. The wind came in, and with it the smell. He took a deep breath, and smiled. It wasn't exactly rose petals, he thought, but it does bring me back… He rolled up the window again, and suddenly felt mildly excited. He hadn't felt like this during the whole trip up, knowing he was going there, but that smell … He sighed again. It brought him back. Back to his childhood. Back to his roots. Back to where he belonged … Suddenly he wanted the journey to be at an end. To get to where he was going. To get back.

They had decided to leave three months later, when the factory closed for the Summer break. That way they would have some extra cash to be getting along with until they got themselves sorted out in London. It was a sensible decision, but it was a decision that had sad consequences.

They were due to leave in a week. They had handed in their notice at the factory, their families were informed, they were ready to go, and there was now no turning back.

Jim could see it on his face, even before he came to sit down at the table in the pub. It was haggard and drawn, and he could see the pain in his eyes. "What's wrong, Harry?" he had asked, showing genuine concern. "You look terrible."

It was the old story. How many others had sat through a similar conversation through the years? And how many others would do the same in years to come? But the timing couldn't have been worse. "Maureen's pregnant," Harry told him quietly. "I can't go with you. I'll have to stay." And his eyes had fallen to the table and remained there.

He had tried to reason with him. "She can come down when we've got ourselves settled," he had said. "We'll find a place that's big enough for all of us. And the baby …"

But it was no use. In those days, if you got a girl in trouble, you did the right thing. It was expected of you, he thought, as he crossed the river, glancing down at the boats moving on it. He really had no choice, he acknowledged. Harry was always a good kid. He always did the right thing, he thought, as he turned the car east along the northside of the river.

And he had also had to make a choice. To cancel all the plans they had made, and stay. To try to get his job back again. Or to leave as planned, but now alone. He had never really wanted to leave. That had been Harry's dream, not his. So he had decided to stay. But fate took a hand. The job was gone, so the choice had been made for him, and he had taken the train early one morning twenty years ago, with a strange feeling of being sent into exile, against his will.

He looked at the streets and building he passed, and the people moving by him. You should have come with me, Harry, he thought. You should have got out of this place when you still had the chance. Now it's too late.

He turned a corner and drove into a side street. It hasn't changed much, he told himself quietly, looking at the blackened brick buildings and the obvious poverty of the place, with a grim expression on his face. Then he smiled, for no particualr reason. Still, it was good to be back, he thought, and felt glad to be there.

Half-way down the street he stopped at the curb and got out of the car. He locked it, and stretched his back. His gaze went up and down the street, then came back to the house before him. Nr. 17. God, how many times had he knocked on that door in his life? he thought. "Is Harry coming out to play?" How many times? "Coming out for pint, Harry?"

He smiled at the memory, and knocked twice, like he had always done. The door opened slowly and a figure came into the opening. He had aged. His hair was long and grey and his face had become thin, the skin had a yellow hue to it that had never been there before. The eyes were tired and sad.

"Morning Harry," Jim said and held out his hand.

"Hello Jim." The voice was dead.

They shook hands, and went inside, closing the door behind them.

Do you Remember, Do you Recall 1966

- The last official performance by The Beatles (In San Francisco)
- England beat West Germany 4–2 to win the World Cup. Geoff Hurst got a hat-trick and a place in the history books
- Spy George Blake escaped from Wormwood Scrubs
- Walt Disney of Mickey Mouse fame died
- Vivien Leigh – the only Scarlett O'Hara there could be – died, leaving Tara to its fate
- Jane Fonda tried to keep Lee Marvin and his horse sober in Cat Ballou
- Michael Caine was Alfie, and seemed to enjoy it
- Peter Sellers and Peter O'Toole partied their way through What's New Pussycat?
- The Hills Were Alive to the Sound of Music with sweet Julie Andrews and stern Christopher Plummer falling in love to Rogers and Hammerstein

Some popular records that went right to the top:
- Good Vibrations: The Beach Boys giving us good vibes
- Eleanor Rigby: The Beatles with cellos and a song that became an instant classic
- Yellow Submarine: The Beatles with Ringo on vocals for a change, and it worked!
- Strangers In The Night: Frank Sinatra proving he could still do it.
- You Don't Have To Say You Love Me: Dusty Springfield singing like only she could
- The Green Green Grass of Home: Tom Jones wishing he was there.

"The long and winding road that leads to your door …"
The Long and Winding Road (Lennon & McCartney)
The Beatles "Let It Be" LP 1970

The Long and Winding Road

She was waving to him, happy to see him again, with a wonderful smile of pleasure on her face, welcoming him back. She held the baby against her body with her free hand, and for a moment the memory of its innocent face crossed his vision before he again focused on the warmth of the welcome before him. He smiled. He was a lucky man to have such a woman. He could feel the warmth of her embrace and smell the sweetness of her skin as he held her tight and burrowed his face into her, kissing her cheek and neck and throat, pressing her against him and never wanting to let her go.

She was still waving to him when an angry car horn jerked him back to reality, and he turned his head to the side mirror and watched as the Aston Martin accelerated and passed him, moving ahead and obliterating the vision where his wife and baby only a moment earlier had been waiting for him. Now they were gone.

He sighed and stretched his back, then moved his buttocks to get a more comfortable position in the seat. He checked the traffic behind him. A few cars and a couple of other lorries, but no more than to be expected; After all few people wanted to be on the road on Christmas Eve. Like him, those who were travelling would undoubtedly be on their way home to be with their families at Christmas.

He cast a glance at the sky. It looked like it might be a white Christmas, he thought. That would really be something …

111

He stared at the road ahead, and, without consciously thinking about it, began to groan out the words to the old Bing Crosby song. It wasn't good listening, even for him, but it kept his mind occupied for a few moments and the sound of his own voice gave him company as long as it lasted. The song came to an end. White Christmas by all means, he thought, but not before I'm home. No snow on the road when I'm driving, thank you very much!! And he raised his eyes to the heavens, making sure that they had got the message.

He had been on the road for five years, hauling rolled steel from the north to the south and whatever they had for him on the way back. It was a lonely life, and he sometimes felt like the captain of a ship with the responsibility of cargo and vessel resting on his shoulders. But he had no crew to share it with. No one to talk to. Only himself. He sometimes surprised himself by the sound of his own voice talking where there before had only been the straining of the engine to fill the silence in the cabin. "You're becoming daft" he would then tell himself. Then add "Senile". "Stupid." And he would continue in the same way, finding alternative adjectives to describe his first statement, using the exercise to help pass the time. When he couldn't think of anymore, he summarised his thoughts with one word. "Thick," he thought. "That's what you are. Thick!"

A smile crossed his face as he played with the words in a new exercise. "You're thick," he said aloud. Then added, in another voice, "Yeth, doctor, and I need a nurth to help me with my thekth life. It'th not ethpethially thukthethful". He grinned to himself. "Thatth life!" he said in his own voice, and chuckled.

Long distance driving was a boring life, always on the way to somewhere but never really getting there. But it did pay his rent and keep his family, so he put up with the boredom, the long lonely hours and the sadness he felt every Monday morning when he had to leave home for another week on the road, away from the warmth of his family.

Whenever his friends asked him how he felt about it, he would just shrug his shoulders and reply that life was just a long and winding road, and he was at least travelling along it in style, sitting on a good seat. "Anyway, it pays the rent, and it always brings me home in the end," he would tell them. And that was the only thought that kept him going from the moment he climbed into the cab early on Mondays, until he locked the doors on the same cab on Friday afternoons: "I'll soon be home again". And he would count the days, then the hours, as the week slowly passed, until he was finally back home again with the woman he loved.

The down side was that, once home, he also counted the hours, until he would once more have to leave, dreading the moment as it came closer, and knowing that it always went much too quickly.

There was a long stretch of road before him, and he watched as another lorry, moving slightly faster, began the slow process of passing him. As it came to his side he exchanged a smile and a wave with the other driver. He looked ahead and saw a car speeding towards them flashing its lights at them, and he quickly used the brake to reduce his speed and allow the other lorry to pass and get back into the lane. The car pressed its horn as it passed and the driver shook his fist and mouthed a curse at them from an angry face as he sped by. "Twat" he said quietly, then concentrated on the road before him.

He had known her since they were still at school, but it was not until he had met her at a local dance a few years later, that he had really noticed her. In the few short years since leaving school she had blossomed into a beautiful young woman, and he had become attracted to her and had become part of the competition to claim her interest. They had gradually found each other, and had gone through the joys and traumas of falling in and out of love, before they had finally acknowledged that they wanted to spend their lives together, and had married.

He smiled at the memory. She had been a beautiful bride. Made him proud, she had. It had been a fantastic wedding and he had spent the day floating on air, and unable to keep his eyes from her, and the night in her embrace. He remembered lying on his side watching her as she slept, while the warmth of his feelings for her almost overwhelmed him.

The honeymoon had been short and hectic, and the departure from her for a new week on the road had been heartbreakingly difficult, but he had had to go. This was his job. This was what paid the rent, and now that they were married they needed it even more than before. Although the parting had been hard, and the week spent away from her painful, the joy of reunion at the end of the week had quickly made them forget their misery, and they had spent the weekend in each others arms making up for lost days and nights. A new honeymoon. But also this time, a honeymoon that was too quickly over, and before he knew it, he was back on the road again, already missing her even before turning on the engine and releasing the clutch to set the lorry in motion.

The baby had come six months ago, and they had been ecstatic. He had become increasingly concerned as her time approached, not only from the normal worry of something going wrong, but also because he was afraid that he would be on the road somewhere, unable to be there for her when she needed him most, and he would nervously call from a phone box several times a day to check on developments.

He had made a call from outside London one evening in May, when her sister had answered. She had just been taken to the hospital. He had jumped into the cab and driven as quickly as he could through the night, worrying with every mile about everything that might be happening, that might go wrong, and praying to a god he had never really believed in, to please help her, to please make everything allright, then cursing the lorry for its lack of speed as he pressed on as fast as he could make it go.

He had arrived at the hospital, weary eyed and tense, and had run into the ward, just in time for the birth of their first child, and he had had tears in his eyes as he held his daughter for the first time and heard her voice crying out its complaints and demanding her mother's breast. Relief and joy had flooded through him. He had never loved anyone like he loved his wife at that moment, and he knew he always would.

The fact that he had returned without delivering his load had certainly slowed him down as he drove to his wife that night, but his boss had not been slow in letting him know what he felt about it, and he had been sent back south with the same load within hours of holding his child for the first time. However, he had been there. He had been there for her. He had been there to receive his own child. And he whistled with thankful pleasure as he pressed on down the long road back to the south, knowing that his wife and child were safe, and that he had now become the father of a healthy baby daughter. "She even looked like her," he said aloud, and smiled at the memory.

It was becoming dark, so he lit the lights. He saw a transport café ahead and thought of stopping to stretch his legs and have a cup of tea, but decided against it. He wanted to get home; It was the first Christmas they would share as a family, and he still had a long haul before he would be home. Instead, he leaned towards the thermos flask lying on the passenger seat, and filled a cup of tea, sipping it as he drove, ignoring the lights of the vehicles coming towards him, and enjoying the anticipation of coming home.

That was the good part, he thought. It's a long road, but it always ends up at home. He had begun to take the positive outlook on his situation after he was married. Instead of thinking of the haul as being away from his wife and the comforts of home, he would force himself to focus on the lie that he was really on the way home – even as he was in the process of leaving it.

As he drove through the country, he would drive along short or long straight stretches where he could see for miles ahead, and he would swing the lorry through never-ending winding country lanes, turning the wheels right then left then right again to follow the road. There were flat roads, and roads with steep or mild gradients, sometimes rising before him, other times dropping ahead of him, when he would have to use the gears to climb, or to control the descent. There were dual carriageways where traffic could pass without difficulty, but normally the roads had only two lanes, and any vehicle wanting to pass would have to cross into the oncoming lane, and that would sometimes cause a problem, but it usually went well.

He had once worked out that he drove around sixty thousand miles a year. That's a lot of road, he had conceded. That was when he had formulated the thought that, although it's a long and winding road, it always takes me home, and he would remind himself of that fact several times a day as he droned through the country with only his own thoughts for company.

Not long now, he thought, as he took a left fork that brought him on to a new road. Another two hours and I'll be back home, he thought, then said it aloud, "Another two hours, and I'm home!" and he took a deep breath as though to give himself new energy for the final spurt, after several hours and countless miles had worn at his stiff body and tired mind.

He began to hum an old Pat Boone song. He couldn't remember the words, only the title. So he hummed the tune, then came in with the title where the words fitted, and sang "I'll be home, my darling," with increasing gusto as he repeated the verses, and noticed his mood was becoming exhuberant as he sang, as though the song was bringing him home faster.

He glanced at the presents that lay on the passenger seat in their Christmas wrappings. He had stopped outside London and bought them there. Something for the baby and a new dress for his wife. She had now got her figure back after having the baby, and he smiled to himself as he thought of her reaction when she opened the parcel and put on the dress. She would be a rare sight in it, he thought, then smiled as he said, "But it won't be on for long, if I can help it!"

The night was dark and he was driving through country landscape dotted with small woods that alleviated the boredom of endless fields hedged in from the road. He was driving along a long stretch of winding road, his lights lighting up the trees of the woods ahead of him, then gradually following the turn of the wheel as they negotiated each bend in the road. His thoughts stayed with his family, and the anticipation of coming home, and having their first Christmas together. He pictured them before the fire. She was wearing her new dress and holding the baby, and she was smiling at him. That smile that went straight through him, and made him feel special. He sighed. It would be great to be back home, he thought, and smiled back at the picture in his mind.

A piercing carhorn jerked him awake, and he swung the wheel to swerve back into his own lane, barely avoiding hitting the car that had been coming towards him. Without realising it, he had allowed the lorry to glide too far into the road and slightly into the path of the oncoming traffic. "God, that was bloody close," he said in a shaky voice, and noticed how tense he was. He settled himself into a better sitting position, and forced himself to breath deeply, feeling how it helped his concentration.

As he began to relax again after the initial shock had settled, he admonished himself fiercely. "Bloody stupid bugger!" he hissed, "You could have killed yourself!" He hit the wheel angrily with the flat of his hand. "Then where would they have been?" he asked himself. He had reduced speed after the incident, and now drove more carefully than he would normally have done. He kept talking to himself as he turned the wheel, following the pattern of the dark and winding road. "It's Christmas, for God's sake! Do you want them to become widowed and fatherless at bloody Christmas?!" His face had become angry and the anger was directed against himself; There was nobody else present to do it for him. He finally allowed it to pass with a final insult "You chuff!" he said, then concentrated on the road ahead, driving with care.

The incident gradually passed with the miles, and the miles brought him constantly closer to home. He concentrated on driving carefully, reminding himself that it was more important that he got home at all, rather than getting there a little earlier. His mood relaxed again and he again pictured them before him. Through the darkness of the twisting countryside he could see them smiling and laughing. She waved to him. He smiled and, in his mind, he waved back.

Just as he was returning her wave, the lorry came into a new bend in the road. The lights swept through the darkness straight ahead, always a heartbeat too late to show what was outside the beam where the lorry was moving through the bend. Half way through the bend, the beams suddenly lit up three figures walking right in his path. They did not move, as though blinded and crippled by the light that hit them. There was no time. He stamped hard on the brake and swung the wheel in a desperate attempt to avoid them, pulling the lorry away from them and into the road. The screeching of the brakes and the tires mixed with the screams from his own throat, as he fought for control and the lorry plummeted across the road and hit the trees then rolled over and lay on its side with the wheels spinning in the air, while steam hissed from the engine and the cargo rolled on to the tarmac.

It had only taken seconds. A count from one to five was all it had taken from start to finish. The three pedestrians ran to the lorry in shock and alarm, and stood and watched in helpless and hopeless inactivity as they shouted to each other hysterically.

Another lorry slowed to a halt nearby. The driver jumped out and ran to the cab. He climbed up and, with difficulty, managed to lift the cabin door and open it. He looked inside. "My God!" he exclaimed, then dropped back to the ground.

One of the pedestrians shouted in a panic-stricken voice "Is he dead?"

The driver kept his eyes on the lorry lying on its side with the wheels still spinning, but slower now. "Yes," he said heavily. "Definitely …"

He walked in front of the lorry, feeling the broken glass of the smashed windows crunch under his shoes. He stumped his foot against something on the ground. He looked down and saw a parcel lying there in the beam of the one remaining headlight. He picked it up. The Christmas wrapping had been soiled from the ground, but the parcel was still intact. He turned it towards the light, in order to see the writing better. "To my darling wife" he read, "From your loving husband on the long and winding road".

His eyes lifted back to the lorry where the driver lay mangled and bloody, beyond help. He shook his head sadly, and in a voice that broke as he spoke, he quietly said "Happy Christmas, mate, whoever you are. Happy Christmas …" And a tear rolled down his cheek and glistened there for a moment in the reflection of the beam from the broken lorry, before it rolled away and was gone.

Do you Remember, Do you Recall 1967

- The six-day war between Israel and Egypt (with the rest lurking on the sidelines)
- The Cuban revolutionary Che Guevara was killed in Bolivia
- Beatle-manager Brian Epstein was found dead in his flat in London
- Darling Julie Christie
- Tragically, Omar Sharrif never got Julie Christie, his true love, in Dr. Zhivago. (Whatever happened to Julie? Julie we've missed you!)
- David Hemmings looked like a kid with a Brownie in Blow-Up
- Clint Eastwood looked like he had problems with his piles in A Fistful of Dollars
- Flower-Power and the Summer of Love
- If you remember any more than this, you weren't enjoying life

Some popular records of the year that went right to the top:
- I'm A Believer: The Monkees (Did they, or didn't they actually play on that record? But who cares ...)
- Release Me: Engelbert Humperdinck with the decade's best PR-stunt, when getting slotted on the live Sunday Night At The London Palladium for a supposedly sick Tom Jones. Engelbert was unknown before that performance, but everyone knew him after it. Incidentally, he and Tom had the same manager. What a coincidence ...
- San Francisco: Scott McKenzie as the prophet of the flower-people
- Puppet On A String: Sandie Shaw in her bare feet
- A Whiter Shade of Pale: Procul Harum showed that pop could have class.

"The end of my hopes, the end of all my dreams ..."
No Milk Today (Gouldman)
Herman's Hermits 1966

No Milk Today

Michael Miller was a milkman in the Midlands with a reputation he would have been proud of had he been aware of it. Being preoccupied, however, he wasn't. Instead, he lived in the innocent belief that his life was of no interest to others than himself. He was forty and, quite understandably, divorced. His libidinous nature had never got used to the idea of monogamy, and he therefore never felt the burden of conscience riding him for the pain he caused his wife whenever he used his indisputable charms to make new conquests.

She had taken it as long as she could, and when she couldn't anymore, she had packed her few possessions and left him. It had come as a shock to him at the time, but he had soon got over it. They had no children and he saw no reason why she shouldn't be able to find a new man in her life, although she would be hard put to find one who was as much a man as he was, he assured himself, as a matter of fact.

He had always had a way with women. For some reason they found him irresistable. He had never bothered to consider why, but had been happy to acknowledge the fact and to enjoy the fruits it harvested. It was the thrill of each new conquest that excited him. Getting to know them was the best part. Seeing the interest in their eyes and knowing what they were thinking, and what they wanted, flirting and manoeuvering, seeing how far they would go and how long it would take before they got there. He would love them until he lost interest, and the interest usually waned quickly once the conquest was made. Love them and leave them. As simple as that. And never get involved emotionally.

He never had any qualms about ending a relationship. In fact he never did. There was never any explanation, no consoling words or goodbye kisses. He simply stopped seeing them. One day sharing their bed and the heat of the moment, the next just on nodding terms, as though it had never happened. After all, he had brought some excitement into their drab lives and they had both enjoyed themselves, so they should count themselves lucky for the experience. When he lost interest, he would simply deliver the milk and pick up the empties, as usual, as if nothing had happened. But now with just a nod and a neutral "Morning," before going on his way, as though they had never shared secret passion and with-held restraint, and as though he was unaware of the insecurity and turmoil his sudden lack of interest caused. As though he cared!

They would sometimes react with hushed anger and frustration, hissing at him from the front door like snakes, but afraid to strike, knowing what was at stake if someone was to find out. Homes, marriages and reputations lying in rubble overnight. So he would leave them in simmering and impotent anger, feeling used and discarded, but safe in his silence. "You self-centred sod," one had hissed at him, "You only think about yourself!" He had looked at her uninterestedly, then replied in a matter of fact voice "But you enjoyed it too, Doris, didn't you?" leaving her mouthing air as she tried to search for a reply.

In spite, some would begin to buy their milk from the grocer, leaving out the "No Milk Today" sign, in some meaningless attempt to get back at him. But they would soon get tired of it, and the empties would again appear on the doorstep with their markers for the day's supplies.

Early each morning he would fill the milk float at the dairy with crates of milk and cream, and start deliveries just after the customers had left for work, the float rattling its contents down the lanes and streets as though signalling his arrival. While the men were at work, the wives were alone, and he knew that many had the fantasies of the night still on their minds and tingling their bodies.

Morning was always a good time. Some were coy in their approach. Others blatant. Whichever approach they chose, the meaning and the end result were given. Some would come out for the milk in their dressing gowns, allowing cleavage or a thigh to show, with an inviting "Good Morning" and a look in their eyes that couldn't be mistaken, and he would know that they had woken from sweet dreams still unfulfilled.

He would sometimes be invited in for a cup of tea, and rarely said no to such an invitation, knowing that there would be more than tea to quench his thirst. He knew that they had a long boring day of housework and shopping to get through, alone in the house and alone with their thoughts, and a bit of excitement at the start of the day would help them through it.

He never boasted of his exploits. He never mentioned them to anyone, not even to the few friends he had. They would sometimes joke about his job. "I mean, a milkman's got a woman in every street, just waiting to get some bottle," one had said, but he hadn't commented. Without really being aware of it, he knew that his silence was a necessity for the life he led, and that without it, it would soon come to an end. And, of course, he had to think of the women and their reputations. In his own way he was a cavalier, with principles.

And he did have certain principles. For example, he never allowed himself to have more than two affairs at a time. Among other things, he had to think of his own reputation, and even his stamina had its limitations. So he would content himself with mild flirtation and innuendo with other potential admirers, laying the basis for future invitations for a cup of tea for when he was again ready and available.

"Anything for the customer," he would say, as he caressed them, and the tea would be forgotten until it was cold.

During his years as a milkman he had been moved from one round to another, and back again. Sometimes this had been at the suggestion of some customer, but the dairy had never bothered to ask why, or bothered to inform him of the request. He never queried such changes, being only too happy to have a change of scenery. "New places, new faces," he would say, looking forward in expectant anticipation to the opportunities that would open themselves to him there.

He loved women. But he had never loved a woman. Not even the woman he had married. It had been nice enough to have a woman to look after him and to keep his bed warm, he acknowledged. But he never missed her after she had gone. Women were his life, but there was no woman in his. He didn't mind. On the contrary, he only wanted the freedom he had. He sometimes felt like a sailor, without responsibilty and with a new woman in every port. The only difference was that there was no time wasted sailing between each new port of haven. He knew he would never have made a sailor, the voyage would take too long, and his impatience was too short. He preferred the milkfloat to a boat; it might not be as romantic, but it got him into port, and a lot faster.

He looked upon each delivery as a port of call. Each house a place where he could tether his moorings, and each woman inside it as a woman waiting, for him. Although the great majority of customers were unaware of his escapades, and thought of him only in terms of the milk he supplied, with a round that covered three hundred houses, there would, nonetheless, always be enough willing women waiting. It's a case of percentages, he would sometimes think, there'll always be someone looking for a bit of loving. You just have to catch them at the right time, when they're ready and randy.

It wasn't the sex in itself. Oh yes, he loved every moment and took it to the limit, feeling obligated to give full satisfaction, making sure that he left them wanting more. But the thrill of the chase, knowing that they wanted it, but knowing also that they wanted to feel as though it was they who were being seduced and not the other way around. Wanting to convince themselves that it was not their own needs that had instigated the act, but that they had somehow been coerced into it.

After all, they weren't easy. They weren't loose women. Just lonely. He filled a void in their existence and made them feel wanted. He gave them the excitement they had lost to the long solitary and meaningless days of being housewives chained to the house and its drudgery. Without obligation. As long as it lasted. And that wasn't long.

"You won't tell anyone, will you?" They all said it after the first time. After the second time, they didn't care.

It was always a case of knowing their needs and adhering to them, then taking it one step further. Then another, until there was complete capitulation. And then allowing them to pretend that they had had no part in the proceedings leading up to the passion they shared, as though they had been helpless, with no willpower of their own to ward off his advances. That was fine by him. It was a game. A game that they both played. A game of pretence that they both knew to be false, but that, in itself, seemed to stimulate them even more.

Being a milkman may not in itself have been an affrodisiac to them, but he was available when they needed him and when they themselves had the opportunity, and that was enough to wet their appetites and make him interesting.

He sometimes felt like a social worker looking after the needy. It's a hard life, he would say, but somebody's got to do it, and he would grin at the thought.

A new occupant moved into the bungalow at the end of the lane in the beginning of February. She was in her late thirties, and lived alone with only a Golden Labrador for company. She had a striking appearance, that needed no make-up, fancy clothes or jewellery to enhance it. Everything about her was natural. Her long blonde hair was combed down to her shoulders and swung freely as she moved. The face was open and smiling and the eyes seemed to sparkle.

He had been bending over the bottles on her step when the door had opened and he had looked up and seen her for the first time, standing over him with a smile on her face and a request for some cream. "I forgot that I needed cream," she informed him in a laughing voice. He couldn't take his eyes off her face as he rose from the bottles, then backed towards the float to get it as he watched her bend to pick up her milk.

He tried to make small talk. "You're new here, aren't you. How do you like it?" She answered him, and joined in with her own questions and comments, and they were soon talking easily together, enjoying the odd jocular comment that fell into the conversation. He was enthralled as much by her friendly words and the voice they came from as by the vivaciousness of her face, and the slender figure with its feminine curves.

He didn't want to leave, but the talk ended naturally, and she moved inside and closed the door with a smile and a "See you," and she was gone, leaving him standing on the gravel with the empties in his hand and a blank and empty expression on his face, suddenly feeling inadequate.

She seemed so sweet. He couldn't get her out of his mind. She followed him on the float as he completed the round, hardly noticing that he was doing it. She stayed in his head the rest of the day and through the night, and remained there when he began his round the next day, like a schoolboy excitedly looking forward to seeing her again. He had taken his time at her house, and had made enough noise to be heard, but she had not appeared. Instead of clearing his mind of her, this seemed to glue her even more strongly to it, but now with some kind of juvenile insecurity blending with the picture he already carried there.

The days passed. He had lost interest in the other women on his round, but whenever he did allow himself to be invited in, he found his mind wandering and her face smiling at him, somehow making his present activity seem sordid. "Is something wrong?" one had asked with a curious expression on her face as she lay under him on her bed. The question had startled him back to reality. "No," he had said, then tried half-heartedly to concentrate on the job in hand.

"Is something wrong?" The question had stayed with him, and helped to build a growing feeling of insecurity that he had never before experienced. For the first time in his life he had found a woman that he really wanted, and his days were filled by thoughts of her. He couldn't help himself. She just wouldn't stay away.

She did come to the door once or twice in the next few weeks, and they had again exchanged friendly banter while he wondered how to get a step further in their relationship, but the door had been closed with another sweet "See you," before he had managed to consolidate his position.

Things were now becoming out of control. During an obligatory triste with one of his conquests on the round, he had failed to get an erection. She had been disappointed. He had been horrified. This had never happened to him before. He was shaken, and pulled himself together the next day while determinedly giving it all he could with another customer, to prove to himself that yesterday's failure had just been a one off. "Hey, you're being busy, today," she had told him, as though it was her who was making the rules and controlling the game, and not him. "Yeahh …!" he had said, sourly, then he had quickly dressed and left her with no intention of returning.

Three months after their first encounter she had come to the door as he arrived with the bottles, and the dog had managed to push past her and ran to him with its tail wagging. It had jumped up against him and he had lost a bottle as he tried to keep his balance. She had angrily called the dog to her, then showed her concern. "I'm sorry," she said, "Are you allright?"

Never better, he thought as he noticed how she fussed over him. "It's o.k.," he told her, and smiled bravely as he began to wipe the spilled milk from his trousers.

"Come inside," she said, "and I'll find a cloth to clean you up."

They were soon sitting at the kitchen table, talking as they sipped the tea she had made for them. "Do you take milk?" she had asked as she handed him his cup, and they had both laughed. He felt exhilarated, and patted the dog's head in gratitude. In return, the dog placed its head in his lap and stared at him with baleful eyes. "Don't do that Lady!" she admonished it, and pulled it gently away from him.

God, he wanted her so badly! He had never been in love, but if there was such a thing, this must be it, he thought. The reaction in his trousers had shown as she wiped the milk from them with a wet cloth. She must have noticed. "Sorry," he said, without explaining, and was torn between restraint and taking her in his arms. She glanced into his eyes at the sound of his voice. "That's allright," she said, without embarrassment, and took the cloth to the sink and rinsed it under the tap.

For the first time in his life he had no idea what to do. The normal course of events in such a situation would be joking flirtation, followed by more serious flirtation and the first light physical contact, then backing off to give them space, before moving in again with some serious compliments, closer physical contact, suggestive whispers and caresses, all the time building on the need all women have to have their sexual attraction confirmed, and finally, the mutual longing coming together in excited passion as their naked flesh joined.

It had nearly always worked. If not the first time, then the next. If not the next, then the time after that again. If it hadn't worked then, then she would have to do without; he always had other choices who would be willing enough.

But this was different. He had been infatuated by her since the first moment he had set eyes on her. He wanted her. But he wanted more than just her body. However, he didn't know how to go about it. He tried a compliment. "You're a very beautiful, woman," he told her seriously. "How come you're living on your own?"

She smiled a "thank you" at him, then replied simply that she preferred to live on her own. He noticed that she had not been embarrassed by the compliment, and drove on. "It must be a bit lonely, though, living on your own. You must miss having a man about the house," then finished lamely, You know …" and he shrugged his shoulders to finish the sentence.

That smile, he thought, as she smiled again, it keeps coming back. "Not really," she replied, then bent down to ruffle the dog's fur. "I've got Lady to keep me company."

"Lucky Lady," he said, and meant it.

She laughed, then eyed him openly, her eyes twinkling as she spoke. "Why," she asked. "Are you making an offer?"

Was she playing with him, or was this a come-on? He couldn't be sure, but he had to find out. "Any man would give his right arm to be with a beautiful woman like you," he told her honestly. "I know I would." And he gave her the look that had melted many women before. But she only bowed her head in mock gratitude and laughed good naturedly.

His body tensed, and he leaned towards her and spoke earnestly. "I mean it," he told her. "I think you're the most beautiful woman I've ever seen." He moved closer, sitting on the edge of the chair, staring into her face. "I can't stop thinking about you," he admitted, then put his hand out and gripped her arm gently. She didn't remove it. "We all need someone," he said, "and I need you." He felt that he had gone too far, but noticed that she was listening to what he said. His hand was still resting on her arm. He began to stroke it in slow motions. He saw her cast a glance at his hand as it began to move. The smile had gone. Her face was now impassive, as though considering what he was saying and doing, yet not ready to decide how to respond. "Any man would," he finished, then lowered himself towards her, and kissed her gently on the mouth expecting to be pushed away, but experiencing no resistance to his advance.

He moved his hand towards her breast, but her own hand gripped his and held it. He noticed her other hand stroking up his thighs, and he tensed at the unexpected touch. "You're excited," she whispered. It was impossible to hide the fact.

"I want you," he mumbled, and his whole body trembled with the strain of holding back the intense excitement that was almost overpowering him. He had dreamed of her night and day for months. Longing for her. Wanting her. And now she was in his arms, willing and eager and about to be his …

The telephone exploded into his mind, ringing harshly from the hall. She pushed him firmly away from her, gave him a sweet smile – God, how she could smile! – then she got up and took the phone. "Yes … Yes … No … Not today … Perhaps next week … We'll see … Allright … Bye!" and the phone was back on the hook. He had followed her to the phone. As she spoke he had stroked her arms and buttocks, sides and belly. He had lifted the hair to kiss her neck, and she had let him do it, without allowing it to distract her from her conversation.

He turned her towards him and closed to kiss her, but she pulled away. "No," she told him good-naturedly. "Not now," and she moved away from his embrace leaving him surprised and unsure of himself. He went to her, but she moved easily away, picking up the dog's leash and the keys lying on the table. "I have to take the dog for a walk," she told him, and smiled as she walked towards the front door and opened it to let them out.

He followed slowly with a puzzled look on his face, wondering what had just happened. One moment embracing, caressing, building up to passion, and the next, out of the door and back on the gravel, looking bewildered and feeling it.

She closed the door behind them and walked away, calling to the dog to follow her. "See you!" she shouted back at him, and smiled, as though nothing had happened. She skipped down the drive-way while playfully fighting with the dog, then passed behind the high hedge hiding the lane beyond it, and she was gone.

He stood for long time staring at the gate through which she had just passed. His mind was in a turmoil, yet somehow, empty. He couldn't fathom it. What the hell had just happened? She had built him up, then pricked his balloon to let all the air out and let him fizzle away to nothing. All in a few incomprehensible moments. He didn't understand it. He *couldn't* understand it! But he knew that he now wanted her more than ever.

For the remainder of the day, and through a shiftless night, his mind wandered from insecurity and desperate attempts to comprehend what had happened to him, to the memory of her face, her voice, her touch and the smell of her skin. She had become a part of him that he was unable and unwilling to cut out. He was besotted by her. She was with him all the time. He couldn't concentrate. His mind was too full of her. There was no space for anything else.

He finally arrived at her doorstep the next morning, expectant and hopeful, and longing to see her.

There were no bottles there. Only a sign. "No Milk Today" it said, and his shoulders sagged at the sight of it. He rang the bell, but there was no response, and he eventually slouched back to the milkfloat, got into the seat, pressed the accelerator and drove on to the next delivery, feeling like a broken man.

The sign was still there the next day. There was no response to the bell.

"No Milk Today!" he snarled. "Is she telling me something, or has she stopped taking milk in her frigging tea!" He became despondent. No woman had treated him like this before. It wasn't fair! He could have any woman he wanted, but he only wanted her. And the more days that passed without seeing her, the more he wanted her, and the more he wanted her, the more she dominated every breathing moment of his life. She had become an obsession, and she was tearing him up, squeezing the life from him, turning him into a zombie.

He had lost all interest in other women. They meant nothing to him anymore. All invitations were brushed off with no attempt to hide his lack of interest. He would go to her doorstep every day, like a lost puppy coming home, hoping to see her, but all that met him was the same sign "No Milk Today", and he would once more trudge back to the float, feeling his self esteem waning with each new day, and the burden of uncertainty wearing him down.

He saw the dog once or twice playing in the back garden, but although he looked, he never saw her. And there was never a response to the bell he rang like a hopeful young schoolboy, feeling inadequate and silly, and wondering what he would say if she did come to the door.

The weeks passed. Then the months. She never left his mind. The willing women waiting impatiently on the round waited in vain. He was no longer interested. He had lost all interest in them. And, he thought ruefully, they wouldn't have got much pleasure from me now anyway, eventually having acknowledged the fact that his sex drive was gone. She had effectively neutered him. He felt like a eunoch in a harem of slags longing for the empress but unable to reach her and without the means to satisfy her should he ever do so.

In spite of the fact that he had despondently come away from her door countless times before without seeing her, he continued to make the trip up the driveway every morning, knowing that this day would be no different from the others, yet unable to pass by without doing so.

Then, on a Monday morning, four months after the fateful day that had turned his existence up-side-down, he came to the doorstep and saw that the sign was gone. His heart skipped a beat. There were two empties on the doorstep. He was flustered and suddenly excited. He moved to press the door bell, but the door opened before he reached it. He opened his mouth to speak, but stopped the words before they came, as he saw her come out, pulling a coat over her shoulders and chatting to the man who followed her through the door.

The man nodded to him, then took her by the arm as they passed by him in jovial conversation. She gave him a smile as she walked by him. "See you," she said pleasantly, then snapped her fingers for the dog to come to heel, and he watched as they walked away without a backward glance, holding hands as they passed into the lane, the dog trailing behind them with its tongue hanging out.

"Cause this land's the place I love, and here I'll stay ..."
Ferry Cross The Mersey (Marsden)
Gerry & The Pacemakers 1964

Ferry Cross the Mersey

The murky waters of the Mersey swirled by the bow as the ferry closed towards the pier on the Birkenhead side of the river, the dirty brown water lathered white in its wake by the churning propellor. A light wind, in gentle discourse with the tide, formed small choppy waves that rose and fell away as quickly, and might have passed for a shoal of salmon moving high in the water. However, there had been no salmon in the river in man's memory. The pollution from the various chemical plants further up the river had effectively held them at bay for generations, and the sewage that bled into the murky waters from the towns hugging its banks, did nothing to dispell the tragic fact that the river was dead. Now it was nothing more than a means of transport from inland to the sea, with no other life in it than that which passed through it in the form of the ships moving up and down-river with their various cargoes.

It was a dirty river, hemmed in by the outline of the grimy buildings of Birkenhead on one side, and the dark and foreboding outline of Liverpool closing down on it from the other, with the Liverbirds, perched high on their pedestals, looking down on their domain in mute and lofty disdain.

But Les Baker loved it. It was his river. He had grown up along its banks in a back street off Scotland Road only a stones throw away from it, and the river had been his companion and his playground since he could walk.

The children would fish in it. If they got any fish at all, they would hardly be more than tadpoles, unedable sewagefish, but it was the joy of fishing itself that passed the time and gave them pleasure. They would build small rafts and paddle or sail around the shore area in them, making sure that they stayed close to the bank, knowing, even then, of the dangers from the tides and the current, and respecting the river for its strength.

They would swim in the dirty water, ducking and diving, and not caring about the colour of the water, or the dirt in it, and unaware of the pollution it held. They could spend hours just throwing stones into the water, enjoying each others company and feeling a part of the breeze and the river's sluggish movement. Often they would just sit on the bank following the movement of the water, and discussing the ships that passed by them, guessing at their destination in some distant land, and dreaming of the adventures awaiting them there.

The river was his lifeline to a wider horizon, and spurred the imaginations of his mind. He loved the smell of the sea that followed it from the estuary, somehow confirming for him, that there actually was an endless world of oceans, lands and peoples beyond it, waiting to be explored, and opening itself to him from the mouth of the estuary he could make out from where he stood.

He had had a happy childhood in spite of the wretched conditions in which his environment existed. However, he never reacted to the fact that they were poor and lived under unenviable conditions, quite simply because he had never known any other life. He was therefore unaware of the fact that they were poor, and enjoyed his life as it was, having known no other, and happy to be living it.

His father had worked on the ferries crossing the river since he had left the navy after the war. He claimed that he had never missed life on the ocean and that working on the ferry was like heaven compared to hell. "The pay's nothing to brag about, but at least we don't get torpedoed on the way to Birkenhead," he would say if anyone should ask.

Les had started working on the same ferry when he left school a few weeks before his fifteenth birthday. That had been twelve years ago. Since then he had crossed the river countless times, enough times to make most people sick of it. But Les never tired of the river, and looked forward to each new day on the ferry with genuine pleasure.

The river could be a false lover and a vicious adversary, and many had died through the years in its waters, unaware of its strength and unpredictability. The sandbanks that built up under the surface would find new locations as though to test the fortitude of the ferrymen and their ability to adjust to the changing moods of the river and find their way past them. The current was heavy and volatile and the tides high, and when the wind blew up from the Irish Sea in the west or from up-river in the east, the waves would go high, and the ferries, however solidly they had been built, and no matter how strong the power of the engines, would splash, rise and fall, dip and roll, as though they were toy boats in a North Atlantic storm, being challenged by the elements, not infrequently with fatal consequences for those who dared to accept. Being ferrymen, their pride never allowed them other than to meet the challenge head on.

Les loved it all, the thrill of the challenge, the relaxing pleasure of the calm, the anticipation of each new day, each new crossing and each new ploy that weather or moody river could find to use against them. He knew every current that swirled through the water, every wind that broke the surface, every light and every sound coming through the darkness of night or the eerie uncertainty of mist or fog pressing around them. The fog-horns moaning like great wounded animals, the bells sharply clanging out their warning, and the heavy pounding of engines all around them. He knew them all, and could name the boats and the tugs and the ferries to which they belonged. He felt part of the river as though its filthy waters ran through his veins and gave him life.

He had never offered the dreams of childhood a thought. Faraway places with all their enticements all held one major drawback; they were far away from where he belonged, and he belonged on the river among the people he knew. He was happy and content, and therefore had no reason to dream of another life. Dreams were for the discontented, and he was content with the life he led.

He had met Mary on the ferry. He had noticed her the first time she came on board, but had not had a chance to talk to her then. However there were to be numerous opportunities as she crossed from her home on the Wirral to an art school in Liverpool every day, and they were soon on speaking terms.

She came from a nice home in a country village twenty minutes by bus from the ferry terminal, and was not an obvious candidate for a ferryman from the slums of Scotland Road, but they soon found themselves dating on a regular basis, and gradually falling in love.

The relationship had not been welcomed by her parents. They had tried to make them part, but had eventually had to accept the inevitable. Mary became Mrs. Baker in a wedding ceremony that brought the pride and infectious optimism of the common man, and the sturdy concern of the middle-class together, in what began as a stand-off between the two families warily eyeing each from opposite ends of the venue, and ended in an informal gathering enjoyed by all.

Although both families still remained wary of each other, the one certain that the other considered them below their status, while the other expected to receive a request for financial assistance at any time, they managed to get along in a genuine attempt to accept each other as they were. However, Les and Mary let them live their lives as they would, and concentrated instead on their own, making their home in a flat, and building their own relationship on the happiness they found in each others company.

Like many young people in Liverpool at that time, Jeff had bought a guitar at an ealy age, and had soon formed a group with some of his friends. They were not particularly good, but perserverance and the pleasure of playing together, gradually made them better, and they eventually got bookings in dance halls and small clubs. The fees were pathetically low, but they had enjoyed playing together, so they didn't really care. After all, they were all working and had their wages to get them through the week.

An unexpected offer to play in Hamburg caused some problems. Jeff wasn't willing to risk his job on the river for a two week adventure abroad, but agreed to go with the band when the skipper arranged for him to take his holiday in the same period.

He never regretted going. Although it was long hours of hard work for shillings, and the accomodation made his own home seem like a palace, they had had a good time, managing to make the stay more a hard-working holiday with booze and birds and a lot of laughter. But he was glad to get back to reality when it was over, and feel the throbbing of the ferry under his feet and the breeze on his face as he once again looked across the river to the other side.

This was the crazy time. The Beatles, Gerry, and all the other groups that had shaken the record industry in London from its lethargy, had also panicked them into believing that anyone in Liverpool with a guitar had to be signed before someone else did it. Recording people came up from London and swarmed through the clubs and dance halls, intent on finding new groups to compete with the old.

Les's band happened to be there, and that seemed to be enough for one of the recording people. Before they knew it, they had been offered a recording contract with one of the smaller companies, and two weeks later they went to London for the day, driving down during the night, and returning to Liverpool late the next night, after having recorded a few tapes in a studio. Then back to work.

The record had come on the market a month later, and the record company arranged for them to appear on a television show, and to join a theatre tour through the country to promote it. He had felt guilty at letting his friends down, but had nonetheless no doubt that his decision was the right one. He wasn't a musician. He was a ferryman, and that was all he ever wanted to be. He left the group, and was replaced by someone else.

He never regretted his decision, or was envious of their success when the record went into the lower regions of the charts. He contented himself instead with a feeling of pride at having played on the record, without giving a thought to the money or the fame that he might have had. And he was proud of his friends when they continued their success with three more records that all sold well.

But he was happy, and that was all that mattered. And he felt a pride of his own, knowing that he controlled his own destiny and had chosen to harness it to the river he loved and knew. People would sometimes ask in disbelief why he had thrown fame and fortune away to work on the ferry, but he would just smile. He would shrug his shoulders and tell them simply, "You wouldn't understand." And he was right; they couldn't.

He was no longer part of a group, so he no longer played. On a warm summer sunday when he was off work, he would nonetheless sometimes take his guitar with him on the ferry to New Brighton, and sit in the sun on the deck among the passengers, getting them to join in, all singing their way to the fairground down-river, then back again to the pierhead in Liverpool, and just doing it for fun. Cruising on the river he loved with the sun on his back while playing his guitar to the sound of the voices around him singing with him, and Mary sitting next to him smiling.

Life couldn't be better.

This was were he belonged. He knew it. These were his people, and he was one of them. His river, and his life, and he would never change it. The river would still be here when he was gone, but a part of him would always be there with it, following the tide as it turned, and floating on the breeze it brought with it. He was a ferryman and proud of the fact. This was his river, and he would never leave it.

He turned to Mary, and returned her smile.

Life was good.

Do you Remember, Do you Recall **1968**

- Civil-rights leader Martin Luther King was shot in Memphis, but the dream lived on
- Robert F. Kennedy was shot in Los Angeles while campaigning for the presidency
- Richard Nixon won the election in USA and Tricky Dicky could turn on the tape
- There were student riots on the Continent
- The Soviets occupied Czechoslovakia
- Bruce Reynolds, the last of the Train Robbers, was arrested in Torquay
- Ten thousand people demonstrated for catholic rights in Londonderry
- Jacqueline Kennedy married greek shipping tycoon Aristoteles Onassis
- Dustin Hofmann was The Graduate who slept with Mom but loved the daughter
- Faye Dunaway and Warren Beatie teamed up as Bonnie & Clyde – What a pair!
- Lee Marvin led the Dirty Dozen to war

Some popular records of the year that went right to the top:
- What A Wonderful World: Louis Armstrong made us feel that it was
- Jumping Jack Flash: Rolling Stones – What a gas, gas, gas!
- Hey Jude: The Beatles with a new anthemn for the masses
- Those Were the Days: Mary Hopkin with a song that made us feel something
- Lilly the Pink: The Scaffold having fun with something different.

"Desmond had a barrow in the market place, Molly is the singer in a band ... "
Ob-la-di Ob-la-da (Lennon & McCartney)
The Beatles "The Beatles" LP 1968

Ob-la-di Ob-la-da

The couple walked through the market, stopping once in a while to look at the merchandise on the stalls. As always they had dressed for the trip into town. His tie was knotted tight against the collar of his white shirt, and his jacket was buttoned. The cap on his head was chequered. In spite of the summer warmth, she had her coat on, and a hat on her head. She held her handbag in her left hand, with her right hand resting across it as she walked. He held a bag with the contents of the morning's shopping inside it.

They stopped by a stall and considered the merchandise.

"Can I help you, luv?" The woman behind the stall smiled at him.

He raised his eyes to her.

"Yes, please," he said. "I'll have two pounds of the Granny Smiths." His eyes stayed on her face as she began to fill a paper bag with the apples, uncertainty creeping into the eyes and showing in a frown as he studied her.

"Excuse me," he said, "but don't I know you?"

She smiled back at him. "You do now, luv," she replied.

"No, no." He shook his head. "I'm sure I've seen you before," he insisted, "but I can't place you."

She handed him the bag. "You've probably seen me around," she replied. Then added jokingly: "Are you trying to make a pass?"

He glanced at his wife, then returned his attention to the woman before him. "Of course not," he told her with a hint of embarrassment.

141

"What a shame,"she said, and smiled again. "And just when I thought I was on to a good thing!" She made a face of disappointment. "One and sixpence please," she said, and gave him a new smile.

He noticed the clear honest eyes, and the open expression on her face, and realised that she was only being friendly. He found his wallet and handed her a pound note, then kept his eyes on her face as she found the change, still frowning and wondering where he knew her from.

She handed him his change. "There you go," she said, "eighteen shillings and a tanner, for you, luv." She winked at him. "And promise to be nice to my apples." A smile spread across her face as she spoke. Then she turned to a new customer.

The couple glanced at each other as they wandered away from the stall. They turned to look over their shoulders at the woman they had just left, and uncertainty again showed on the man's face. They exchanged a word or two, shrugged their shoulders, and walked away towards the exit.

A man came up behind the woman, and slid his arms around her. "Get off, Des!" she told him good-naturedly, then let herself be embraced as he held her close and gave her a friendly kiss on the cheek.

"Another one bites the dust" he said, and chuckled. "They're going to be wondering about you all day," he said, then caressed her hair. "You naughty girl, you!" She gave him a warm smile in reply, and absentmindedly began to whistle *Danny Boy* as she picked up an apple and began to polish it.

Des had always worked at the market, taking over the stall from his father when he had finally decided to retire. It was the only life he knew, and the only life he needed. He was his own man and could be himself and do as he pleased; no pretence, no knuckling down for any bosses – what you saw is what you got, warts and all! He loved the life he led, preferring, like his father before him, to call himself a barrow boy, rather than the more refined "market tradesman" that others had begun to aspire to when called upon to explain their vocation in life. He was happy, and it showed through his personality and charm.

It was these aspects more than any other that had attracted Molly to him a few years earlier, when she had met him at a local club where she had been singing with the band. It hadn't taken them long to decide that they enjoyed each others company, preferring to be together rather than apart. They laughed a lot, they smiled and joked and talked and loved and lived together, and had eventually married when she had become pregnant with their first child.

She had joined him in the market soon after they had become an item, and she had enjoyed the bantering and the bartering, the natural intimacy of the environment among the stall owners, naturally open and free-spirited people who spoke their minds, and always had a smile and a good one-liner just waiting to get out. These were her kind of people, and she had blended with them from her first day at the stall.

Des had encouraged her to keep singing with the band, as she obviously enjoyed it, and he would always be there with her whenever they were able to get bookings, which was usually only at weekends. The money wasn't good. It helped, but she didn't do the bookings for the money, but for the pleasure it gave her. "Anyway, Moll," he would often tell her, "You're a bloody good singer, so sing!"

The bookings with the band were now only pleasant memories of the past, but she would sometimes still get up and sing with them if she found herself in a club they were playing. But the band was the past, and this was the present.

He carried her suitcase onto the train and made sure she was comfortable, then took her in his arms and kissed her. "I'll miss you, Moll," he told her, and she whispered "I know. Me too," in his ear. He left the carriage, and closed the door. Molly leaned out from the open window, and they held hands as he walked alongside the carriage while the train began to move away. "Look after the kids when I'm away," she told him unnecessarily. Then added in a louder voice to make herself heard above the sound of the wheels "See you in a few days, luv," as the hands parted, and she blew a kiss at him. She went back to her compartment and settled in the seat with a magasine for company.

The train pulled into London four hours later, and Stan, the company chauffeur came running to relieve her of the suitcase she was carrying as she climbed down to the platform. "Come on, Miss," he said anxiously, "That's my job." He took the suitcase from her, "You shouldn't be doing this yourself."

"Nice to see you again, Stan," she said, and gave him a kiss on the cheek. "What's the matter. Don't you think I can carry my own suitcase?" she asked, and smiled at him fondly.

It had always been the same procedure every time she came to London. At least it had been since her records had begun to sell well, and she had become a national celebrity. That was when they had begun to send Stan to pick her up. They had wanted to send him north to bring her down in the Jaguar, but she had refused. "That's too daft," she had told them, "I'll take the train." And that is what she had done then, and since. And Stan had been waiting each time, and had admonished her each time, when she had carried her luggage from the train before he had had a chance to reach her.

The record executives and her management had not considered it a good idea to travel alone and by train. "You're a star, for gods sake," they told her. "You should be travelling in style." To which she had simply informed them that she enjoyed taking the train "No rush traffic to bother about, and I can stretch me legs."

They had also been concerned about her safety. It could be dangerous for a celebrity to travel alone on public transport, they had told her. People would bother her and she could be accosted, even hurt. "Nobody's going to accost me," she had told them. "Do you think I look like a tart or something?" She had smiled as she said it, but they had hurriedly assured her that that was certainly not the case, afraid of insulting her, and unaware that she was teasing them, and fully aware that their concern for her was only commercially motivated.

"Anyway," she had insisted, "nobody recognises me without the wig and the makeup and all the trimmings, and I'm not about to get up and sing in the bloody corridor, now am I?" What she did not say was that she preferred to be among ordinary people, doing ordinary things with them, and being a part of their lives.

"But what if someone should recognise you?" one of the executives had asked, hardly hiding the frustration in his voice.

Without hesitating she replied, in a matter of fact voice. "I'd just say, "How are you, luv. Sit down, and have a cup of tea". Then we'd have a nice chat, and I'd have some company, and the trip would go much quicker."

"I'll be your star whenever I'm performing," she had told them later. "I'll be Melody Lane at the concerts, the premiers, the interviews, the photo sessions, and all the rest of the ballony. But when I'm not doing all that stuff, I want to be a part of real life. Then I'm just plain old Molly from Liverpool, and I'll take the bloody train like anyone else!"

Then she had given them a sweet smile. "But thank you for caring." And she had curtsied primly.

They had stopped trying then, and accepted the facts of life; their star performer would be arriving by train whether they liked it or not. They didn't, but what could they do?

After checking into the hotel she walked to the studio round the corner. She was casually dressed and relaxed as she entered the foyer. The doorman touched his cap to her, and smiled. "Good afternoon Miss Lane," he offered. "Nice to see you again." He was obviously delighted to see her. She had always had that effect on the people she met; She made them feel relaxed and comfortable, and they were always happy to see her. She had a way of making them feel important to her, and in a way, they all were. She remembered their names and their faces and treated them with respect and as friends.

She smiled at him, "Thank's Bernie, " she said, "Nice to see you, too." She put an arm around his shoulder. "And how's that grandson of yours doing?" she asked. "Still keeping you all up at night, is he?"

Bernie's face lit up. "No," he said, "he's better now. The doctor gave him some medicine, and that did the job." His eyes twinkled as he informed her, "He started walking last week." There was pride in his voice.

She leaned towards him and gave him a kiss on the cheek. "That's just for the baby, when you get home." She made a stern face as she looked into his, "So don't get any wrong ideas, o.k.?" Then they both laughed, and she walked past him with a wave. "See you later," she said. He didn't reply, but the smile on his face confirmed that he hoped he would.

"Darling! There you are!" It was the head of the agency coming towards her with his arms wide. He enfolded her and kissed each cheek. "Darling. So nice to see you again". She noticed how he accentuated "nice", and sighed quietly. It had only been three weeks since the last time, but she didn't comment on the fact.

145

Another figure appeared from the elevator. An executive from the record company. He was dressed in a conservative, striped suit and wore an expensive silk tie adorned with a gold tie pin. He came straight towards her with a huge smile on his face. "Darling. Lovely to see you again!" This time it was "lovely" that was stressed. She sighed again. Another hug and kisskiss on the cheeks. He was already fawning over her, and she hadn't even had a chance to speak. "Hello, Peter." She smiled at him. "It's nice to see you, too," as she wondered "Why can't they relax and be themselves? Another "Darling" and I'll puke!"

"Darling, Melody!" She shut her eyes for a moment, then opened them to see another man in a striped suit. He was standing by the staircase with his arms stretched towards her, his head aschew as he stared into her face with an expression of bliss on his own.

She went towards him and allowed herself to be hugged once again. She decided to play the game. "Darling!" she said in an unnatural and exaggerated voice, "How absolutely wunderful to see you again!" She stressed the u in "wunderful". They didn't seem to notice the sarcasm, so she decided to slag it, and broke into her "orphan of the back-streets of Liverpool" dialect, "Right den, we goin' te stand around huggin' all day darlin', or are we goin' te get some werk dun?"

They laughed. They always laughed when she fooled around. She was their star. She made records that made them millions. So they always laughed. She knew that their laughter would stop the day her records stopped selling; then she wouldn't be funny anymore. "It's all bullshit, you know," she had once told her husband. "They're all over you as long as you're popular, but they'll drop you like last weeks washing when you stop selling records". But she had to admit that they weren't all bad. "I know that they're only trying to be nice," she told him, "but they're so transparent, you can see right through them. You look at some of them and there's nothing there: Just the smile they've painted on the face and the cash register blinking in their eyes."

But she had kept selling. For four years now, her records had regularly entered the charts, and had made her a household name. A star. But that was only in working hours. Outside the limelight she was just Molly. Molly to her friends and family, and Molly in the market where they respected her wish to retain her anonymity, and where she could hide herself away from the pressures of being Melody Lane, and the strain of being fawned upon by people who never seemed to realise that she could see through their shallow pretence, and that it was wasted on her. "Call me a cow, if you want," she would say, "but don't give me all that bull." And they would laugh, not understanding that she really wanted them to treat her as the person she was, and not as the star they had created.

"The money's nice to have," she had once said, "But only because it gives you the freedom to be yourself, and that's all I really want." Then she had added in a serious voice, "And if I didn't have it, I'd still be myself, now wouldn't I?" Then she had smiled to herself as she concluded with the obvious; "So I don't really need it, do I?"

The four days she spent in London were busy. She spent six hours a day in the studio, then became Melody Lane for two personal appearances, a number of interviews, a television appearance on a talk show, and a photo session for the new album. They were long and hectic days, when she played the part she had been given, and she felt relieved when Stan had left the train carriage and she could finally settle back in her seat and relax.

She shared the compartment with another woman and a middle-aged man. They had merely acknowledged each other with a nod and a smile, before hiding behind something to read, only occasionally resting their eyes while gazing into the darkness through the window.

"Excuse me." It was the woman. "You seem very familiar. Have we met?" The look on her face was friendly, but the expression in her eyes was uncertain. "I'm sure I know you from somewhere". The man lowered his newspaper enough to look over it, and studied her face, inquisitive, but only to alleviate the boredom of the journey.

She smiled back at her. "No. Sorry. Don't think so," she replied. "Anyway, how far are you going, luv?" she asked back, and soon the conversation was moving as easily as the train wheels rolling through the Autumn evening, and the time passed quickly as they talked their way through the darkness they passed.

They finally arrived in Liverpool, and began to move to the door. The man opened it and helped the women take out their luggage, just as Des came along the platform and swept her into his arms. "Great to see you again, darling," he whispered in her ear.

"For gods sake don't call me darling, Des. I might think I'm back with those puffs in London." She had her arms around his head squeezing. "Give us a kiss, love, I've missed you, you bugger!" So he did.

"I know what it was!" It was the woman who had shared her compartment and conversation on the way up from London. She tapped her gently on the shoulder, to get her attention, then gave an apologetic smile to the man holding her in his arms, shrugging her head as if to say "Sorry, but I didn't notice". She came back to the business in hand. "I know why you were so familiar," she informed her. "You reminded me of that singer; Melody Lane." She peered into her face studying it. "Did you know you look just like her. The same eyes and the same smile." She pulled her head away, looking uncertain. "You're not Melody Lane, are you?"

She got a radiant smile in return. "Absolutely not." Her eyes found her husband's. They exchanged smiles. She thought about the absurdity of the past four days and the reality of the market stall in the morning, and sighed with pleasure. "I'm Molly," she told her. "Just Molly."

She took Des by the arm, and they walked away, holding each other closely.

The other woman watched them thoughtfully, then nodded her head as though accepting the obvious; She couldn't be Melody Lane. She chuckled at her mistake. "Just Molly", she told herself, "Just Molly", and smiled as she moved along the platform towards the exit.

Do you Remember, Do you Recall 1969

- The Beatles played together for the last time, on the roof of the Apple building. The police stopped the performance. Sacrilege!
- London gangsters, the Kray twins, were jailed for numerous crimes
- Charles became Prince of Wales at Caernarvon Castle to a general shrug of joy
- The Stone's Brian Jones was found dead in his swimming-pool
- Czech student Jan Palach set himself on fire in protest against Soviet occupation
- Neil Armstrong walked on the moon "A small step for man, a giant step for mankind."
- British troops were sent to Northern Ireland to quell riots – and did it help?
- Dwight D. Eisenhower died
- Judy Garland died too soon, but still lives in our hearts Somewhere Over the Rainbow
- Oliver Reed and Ron Moody did Lionel Bart proud in Oliver
- Rosemary's Baby wasn't what she was expecting. (And who is the father …?)
- The Beatles became cartoon characters in the Yellow Submarine
- Woodstock – 200.000 people just there for the love of music and the love of love

Some popular records of the year that went right to the top:
- Honky Tonk Woman: The Rolling Stones still strutting their stuff
- Bad Moon Rising: Creedence Clearwater Revival. Finally someone new and exciting
- Where Do You Go To My Lovely: Peter Sarstedt - intelligent lyrics and haunting tune
- Two Little Boys: Rolf Harris with what was simply a nice song
- The Ballad of John & Yoko: The Beatles ready to call it a day and move on.

"Don't give your love to someone while I'm away …"
Like I've Never Been Gone (Hampton/Monte)
Billy Fury 1963

Like I've Never Been Gone

Dai Jones was finally coming home. He had counted the months and the weeks and the days for a year, but now he was finally on his way back home. Looking back, he realised that time had really gone quite quickly since he had left. But when he had actually been living through it, each day had dragged into the next much too slowly, and time had seemed to move in slow motion without ever seeming to bring him closer to the day he would be demobbed and could go back home to Carol, and the life he had been forced to leave behind him, a lifetime ago.

National Service wasn't a choice he had made, but an obligation that had been forced upon him, like all the other young men of his generation, and the army didn't give a damn about how they felt about leaving their homes and their sweethearts. They only wanted to have the numbers in place, in uniforms that almost fitted, and with minds and personalities that could be manipulated and bullied into submission, to show blind allegience to the army's idea of how a soldier should think, act and be. Which was: don't think, just do what we tell you to do; don't act unless we tell you to, and don't be anything that we don't tell you to be.

They had only been married three months when he was called up. Like everyone else, he knew it was coming, but it still came unexpectedly and certainly very inopportunately. He was just starting life with his young wife, getting used to living together and planning their future. With help from their parents they had been able to rent a small terraced house around the corner from where they had grown up, and had barely had time to get settled in, before the army put him in uniform and shipped him off.

Parting had been hard. How do you say goodbye to someone you love? How can you turn from them, and walk away, knowing that it will be a lifetime before you can come back and hold each other again? How can you leave, not knowing what time apart, alone and lonely, might bring with it of temptations and sorrows? How do you stop yourself from allowing such thoughts to eat into your mind like hungry maggots, infesting it with doubt and insecurity?

It had been hard enough to leave her for the training camp, although they both knew that he would then get leave to enable him to come home to see her. But the second parting had been brutal and heart-wrenching. He was being posted overseas for the duration of his service, and they would not see each other again until it was over. Almost a year apart! It was unbearable. He had managed to hold back the tears, trying to be brave for her, but had instead shared hers, and he had left with the sound of her whimpering sobs in his ears and the memory of her haggard grief-stricken face emplanted on his mind.

On the evening of his departure he had taken her for a ride on his motor-cycle. Feeling the wind in his face and her arms around him had made him feel free from the burdens he carried with him, and allowed him to relax as the miles passed by them.

But when they came back to the house the unremitting truth was again forced upon them; tomorrow he would have to leave her, and the pleasure they had felt as they drove with the wind pulling at their hair, was forgotten, as despondency again sank into them.

He spent two hours in the back-yard, deep in thought and miserable, as he cleaned his motorbike. He had had the Triumph Bonneville for three years, and it was his pride and joy. But now, on the eve of his departure, it meant nothing to him. He was cleaning it just to have something to do, to try to keep his mind off what the next day held for him. God only knew when he would again feel the seat giving under his weight as he sat upon it, or hear the sound of the engine as he turned the throttle, feeling the vibration under his loins.

He gently stroked his hand over the metal and the leather, as though it was a lover, and smiled sadly. He wet a wrag in luke warm soapy water and washed away the dirt, then rubbed it dry with a cloth. He polished the chrome until it shone. He oiled the chain and the brakes and the suspension and every moveable part, then dried it all until the Triumph looked shiny and new in the evening sun. Then he did it all again.

When he was satisfied, he stood back and studied it for a moment as he wiped the dirt from his hands. He found a canvas covering and carefully placed it over the Triumph, taking care to cover it all. He stood for a moment in silence with his head bowed, as though praying over a corpse, while he gazed at it through empty eyes, then looked down at the paving in the yard without really seeing it. He frowned thoughtfully and sighed, then went inside through the kitchen door, and closed it quietly behind him.

They had made their promises before he left. They would be faithful to each other. They would write every week. His absence would not change anything between them. Things would be as before when he returned. It would be as though he had never been away. Like he'd never been gone.

Both had sincerely meant what they had promised, and wanted more than anything to believe that the same applied to the other, but the leech of uncertainty sucked itself into them both and remained with them throughout his absence. After all, they were both healthy young people in their prime, how could either of them avoid temptation when they were world's apart and lonely, without the other to hold?

He knew that she loved him, but how could he expect her to stay faithful for so long, when he wasn't there to fulfill her needs? She was only twenty and couldn't be expected to stay at home watching the television every night. She would go out with her friends to a pub or a dance, and she would meet other men. Men who were on the make. It would soon become general knowledge that she was alone, and that he was out of the running, on another continent, and unable to do anything about their attempts to seduce her to their own designs, using her vulnerability and lack of fulfilment to reach her. How could she remain steadfast for so long. It was almost inhuman to ask it of her, but he did.

"Don't find anyone else when I'm away, Carol," he said miserably, unable to hide the helplessness in his voice. "Please don't. It would really kill me if you did."

She had looked at him steadily as though to print every detail of his face in her mind, while tears whelled up in her eyes. "Oh dear Jesus," she sobbed miserably, and pressed herself against him. "There's only you, Dai," she snivveled. "You know there is. There's only you …"

At her reaction, tears finally found their way from his own eyes and rolled down his cheeks, as he unsuccessfully tried to press them back. "I love you Carol," he whispered hoarsely. "I really love you," and he burrowed his head into her bossom, in an attempt to hide his emotion, and find some comfort there.

He didn't want to go. He didn't want to leave her. It was a forced separation against their will, but there was nothing they could do to stop it. Now they both feared that it would cause irreparable damage to their relationship and their future together, and that it would split them apart, not only when they now would physically be apart, but forever.

The morning eventually came after a sleepless night. They made love, but it was more a desperate parting gesture of love, than passion. They lay in each others arms, holding each other tightly, but not speaking, not knowing what to say. They got up and dressed, then had a hasty breakfast, hardly speaking as they ate. Both knew what the other felt, so there was nothing to say. There was no need for words. A last embrace, long and silent, then he was gone …

That had been almost a year ago, but he could still remember it as though it had been yesterday. He had carried the memory of their parting with him every day and every lonely night, but now the nightmare of their parting would soon be over, and he would finally be coming home again, back with Carol where he belonged.

Throughout his absence they had both kept their promise, and had written every week. Each post delivery had been met with the same expectancy, and the disappointment had been as deep when there had been no letter, as the pleasure had been great when a letter did arrive. Because of the delay caused by the tremendous distance their letters had to travel, two or three letters would sometimes arrive in the same delivery, and that would be a bonus worth waiting for.

Whenever he opened her letters, he would do so slowly, wanting the moment to last, and he would read each letter not once, but twice, then once again. Then he would place them in a bundle with her other letters. During his absence, the bundle grew thicker and became more and more worn as he thumbed through it to re-read the contents that he had already read a dozen times before.

Each letter brought news from home, bringing him closer to it, but more importantly, it brought him closer to her. But they also brought him a feeling of emptiness with the pleasure they gave him. He longed to hold her close to him, to smell the scent of her skin and feel her hair caressing his face. But she was unattainable, like a rainbow that is always out of your reach. So, although her letters brought him joy, they also underlined the fact that she was alone on the other side of the world, in another universe, and that he was helpless to love her, and unable to protect her from whatever demons that might fill his mind with suspicion and despair.

She had kept her promise of weekly letters, but what of her faithfulness? He had no way of knowing, and did not have the confidence to question it, preferring not to know, although this again allowed the questions and uncertainty to prevail in his mind. The pain of pictures conjured up, could make him quail in futile depair, knowing that whatever was happening at home he was helpless to influence it. There was nothing he could do. Only brace himself against the doubts and insecurities that filled his mind every day, and force himself to believe that she was being true to him.

He would then try to focus his mind on the happy times they had shared together. The rides on the motorcycle, as they sped away from the grim reality of the slums in which they had been raised and still lived, into the green of the countryside, with the fields and the hedges and the trees and the river winding its way through them all. The nights in her arms, the sparkle of her eyes as she looked at him and the smell of her when they made love. The secrets they shared with knowing smiles. Sharing the days and enjoying her smile and the sound of her voice. Any man would love her, and that was the dagger that twisted in his chest.

Nonetheless, despite his insecurity, he knew that she loved him, and whenever he was able to accept this as truth, it was like giving oxygen to a drowning man, and he felt the pressure easing from his strained mind, and a sublime feeling of peace and tranquility. Until the demons appeared once more to tease his succeptible fears into helpless panic.

It had been hell for him. But how had their separation been for her? Should he believe her letters, then she had shared his hell and his lonely misery. But how was he to know if it was true? How could he tell? And did he really want to know if it wasn't?

His fear of facing whatever truth that might be lying in the depths of suspicion, was also keeping him from facing the possibility that all his fears and all his suspicions might be groundless and wasted, and that she was actually as miserable and faithful to him as he was to her, and that perhaps, she too was as concerned about his fidelity as he was for hers.

He acknowledged that she had reason for such fears. The other soldiers in his company were happy to enjoy the comforts of the locals, and did so whenever the opportunity arose. He could understand them, and he could not deny that he was also sometimes tempted. But they had both promised to be faithful, and if he expected her to keep her promise, then the least he could do was to keep his own part of the bargain. So he did. The very thought of cheating on her was abominable to him, and the thought of sweating in a local's embrace was abhorrent to him, knowing that she would be with him in his mind, and that it would be a filthy affair in which Carol would be there with him, in the act, while he cheated on her.

She even followed him when he was wading through the jungle on patrol with his rifle at the ready, and he would be more concerned about her reaction to his death, and how it would effect her, than he was for the bullet that might cause it.

But he had survived both the jungle and their separation, and was now finally on his way home.

The voyage back to Europe had been long and uneventful, and only the knowledge that he was on the way home could alleviate the boredom on board the ship that, much too slowly, brought him closer and closer to Carol and the end of their miserable separation. But the pleasure at the thought of their reunion was sometimes marred by doubt. Would things still be the same as they had been between them, or had she changed? Was her affection and love for him as it had been, or had something happened to change them during their separation?

Although the doubts and the questions they raised caused him concern, they could not destroy the pleasure he felt at the prospect of finally being able to hold her in his arms once again, and the anticipation of the moment made him feel warm and happy. God, it would be wonderful to be back with her! He could hardly wait. He would sometimes look out across the vast, empty ocean to the horizon, and think of her waiting for him there, and he would will the ship to go faster, to reach her there.

When they finally arrived in Portsmouth they were given one week's leave before reporting back to base. He had taken the first train north, feeling that the sound of its wheels were chanting to him, over and over again, *I'm coming home, I'm coming home, I'm coming home, I'm coming home …* The words were only in his mind, but the rhythm of the wheels and the knowledge that they were taking him home, formed a song in his heart that was bringing him home to a happy ending.

Or was it? God, don't start thinking, he thought, and forced the old doubts from his mind before they could take hold, then demonstratively began to follow the rhythm of the wheels once more, his mind chanting to it, *I'm coming home, I'm coming home, I'm coming home …*

He had to change trains three times, and lost the last connection and had to wait impatiently for two hours before the next train arrived. She knew he was coming. She knew he would be home that day, but she didn't know when. They had no telephone so he couldn't call her. Instead, he tried to call the local pub. They could give her the message. They could tell her when he would be home. But there had been no answer when he had called. He looked at his watch and realised that they were closed. He swore in exasperation. He had been away too damned long, and had forgotten that the pubs closed at three. One hour too late. Could this be an omen? he thought, then brushed it aside as being ridiculous. The train left five minutes later, and he followed the familiar countryside that passed by his window as his head filled with memories, anticipation, doubts, longing, impatience, new memories and new doubts, and the uncertainty of what he would find when he finally came home to her.

He looked around him at the people in the station as he got off the train, but saw none that he recognised, nobody there to greet him. The disappointment left him feeling empty and uncertain. He brought both with him as he began to walk from the station through the town, the uncertainty growing with each step he took, gnawing at him, competing for his attention with the excitement he felt as he drew closer to his home.

He saw the corner of the street before him, and was swayed between turning back, suddenly afraid of what he might find there, and rushing towards it, running the final steps of the long journey home. Instead, he took a deep breath, steeling himself for whatever was around it, and turned the corner to walk down his street. Their street...

He saw the flag first. The Union Jack had been fastened to the front-room window and was moving gently in the breeze above the pavement. He felt moisture in his eyes at the sight of it, knowing it was for him, and he quickly drew a finger over them to stop the tears before they came. Three more paces along the pavement and he noticed the motorbike. The Triumph was parked just outside their front door, and he could see it polished and shining as though he had never left it. This was also for him. A new tear pressed out on his cheek.

Then he saw the front door opening, and suddenly she was there, as though she had heard him coming. Then she was running towards him with her arms open to him and a radiant smile of joy on her face "Dai!!" she shouted to him. "Dai!!" Then she was in his arms and he could no longer hold back the tears as he squeezed her in a tight embrace, never wanting to let her go, kissing her, smelling her, and only able to whisper her name, again and again, "Carol... Carol... Carol..."

The embrace and the emotion had to end some time, and when it did, they walked slowly towards the house, leaning against each other as they walked, with their eyes glued to each other and happy and contented smiles on their faces.

They stopped for a moment to look at the Triumph, before going inside. They exchanged a glance that said, *Yes, Let's do it*, and he climbed onto the seat, gave the starter a kick and heard the engine roar, and felt it vibrating between his legs. She climbed behind him and he felt her arms holding him tightly and her head pressing against his back. He let out the clutch and accelerated, and they roared through the streets, out of the town and into the countryside feeling the closeness of their bodies hugging against each other and the wind blowing the doubts from their minds. It was a wonderful feeling. Euphoric …

He was back. Like he'd never been gone …

"Though the carnival is over, I will love you til I die ... "
The Carnival is Over (Springfield)
The Seekers 1965

The Carnival is Over

Alice was eighteen and in love.

She had been in love from the moment she had set eyes on him three weeks earlier. Three wonderfully exciting weeks that had filled her with an overpowering feeling of warmth and affection, and had stimulated her body with the exhilarating wonders of a woman awakening. Wonderful days, and exciting nights, running into each other, and making the three short weeks seem like a lifetime.

She was infatuated by him, blinded to all reason and longing only to be in his arms. Even watching him as he worked gave her pleasure, just being close to him, and knowing that they belonged together. Her eyes would light up whenever he found time to come over to her when the Big Wheel was spinning and he had a moment, and she could feel the pride rising in her when he put his arm protectively around her shoulder, as though showing the world that she was his, or kissing her for all the world to see.

He was older then Alice, and his confidence and charm seemed to her, to confirm his maturity. She had noticed him immediately. He seemed to stand out in the crowd as though there was no-one else present. She couldn't keep her eyes from him.

She had gone to the fairground with three friends, and they had enjoyed themselves, lapping up the atmosphere around them, the sounds, the flashing coloured lights, the stalls and amusements, the people milling around, the blaring music. Eddie Cochran and Elvis. Women screaming with excitement as the Dodger rushed through its spiral. Ice creams and candyfloss, and excited voices shouting and laughing. A lot of laughter!

Then she had seen him, and the world had seemed to stop. She had caught her breath, and had held her eyes rivetted on him. Suddenly everything seemed to go quiet around her, as though the volume had been turned down. The noise of the fairground faded away. All movement seemed to slow to shadows of slow motion. The chatter of her friends seemed to dissolve into the background. All her senses were suddenly focused only on him.

He wore a short-sleeved white shirt that showed the tan on his skin, and tight blue jeans that enhanced the lean body. He reminded her of James Dean, only more handsome. The dark blonde hair was thick and wavy, and combed high in front. A cigarette clung to his lips, and the smoke rising from it seemed to form a transparent curtain of blue that gave the face behind it a sensual and mystical aura.

She couldn't keep her eyes from his face as she moved with the queue, as though drawn towards him by some invisible force, and she had trembled slightly as she paid him and heard his voice. "There you are, darling," he said as he looked into her eyes, "Enjoy the trip." He smiled and gave her a wink. "See you when you come down again."

She remembered nothing from the trip on the Big Wheel, only that her eyes never left him, following his movements fom the zenith high above the ground, to the bottom. Round and round, up and down, high and low, her gaze never left him. Whenever he looked up at the wheel she felt that he was looking only at her. He waved and smiled once, and she was certain that they were meant for her.

She had never had a steady boyfriend. Only casual dates with local boys who had failed to interest her in their stinted conversation or platt witticism, and had failed even more miserably in their fumbling attempts to make romance. The little sexual experience she had, had been disappointing; just hopeless attempts at seduction by inexperienced boys with groping hands and panting impatience, who had been firmly pushed away before any damage had been done to either of the combatants.

She liked boys, and enjoyed the experience of becoming acquainted with their desires, but she had never found any boy who could fill her with longing for love and affection, or who could wet her appetite and make her want to give herself to him completely, in a way that only a woman could.

Until now.

It had seemed so easy. So natural. As though it was meant to be.

Although the surroundings had been sordid, the love they had shared in his battered caravan had been divine. No hurry. Time meant nothing. No fumbling. No holding back. No regrets. Just wonderful. Slow and passionate. Again and again.

Whispers. Kisses. Caresses. The smell of his skin. The taste of it. His hair in her eyes. His eyes on hers. Sweat mingling. The moisture from their bodies melting together. Moans in the darkness. From him. From her.

The touch of his hand. The reactions throughout her body. Vibrating uncontrollably. Filling her mind, almost exploding it, with the thrill of a million nerves screaming inside it with pleasure and happiness.

The sound of his voice, low and murmuring. Husky. His breath stroking gently against her ear as he spoke.

It wasn't sex. It was love. It was showing their love for each other. Sharing it.

So natural. So real. So surreal.

So wonderful.

She wanted to lie in his arms forever. Never leave his embrace. Never!

But every night he would walk her home, although late, insisting that she should go home "So your mum and dad don't get worried," he would tell her. And they would kiss again, long and passionately, before he gently nudged her towards the front door, and walked away with a wave, and a hushed "See you tomorrow."

She hardly slept a single night, seeming to float in her bed as she lay under the blankets, her body fulfilled, and her mind flowing over with joy. She was in love. She couldn't help it. She was in love.

They spent every day together. Talking. Holding hands. Exchanging secret smiles that only they knew the meaning of. He worked the Big Wheel, and she would stand close by him as he worked, knowing that, in the unending mass of people coming and going, none could know of the special relationship they shared. It was their secret. They were alone, floating on their own cloud while surrounded by hundreds, but never noticed them, for they only had eyes for each other.

She lay in his arms, her head resting on his chest, feeling the heat from his body. "We're leaving tomorrow," he said, quietly. "I'm going to miss you."

She knew, and bit her lip to stop herself from crying. "I know," she replied in a strained voice, then lifted her head and, in a determined voice, she told him "I'm coming with you."

She stared into his eyes to confirm her conviction.

He stroked her hair gently. "I want that more than anything," he told her. He gazed at her in silence. She turned her head away, and he heard her sobbing quietly. "But you know you can't," he told her.

"I can!" she said defiantly, but the defiance in her voice couldn't hide the misery she felt knowing that it was true. She couldn't just leave her home and her family. She was too young. Too inexperienced. Too insecure.

She was passionately in love with him, and believed as passionately, that he would take care of her, and that they would share their days and remain together. She took it for granted. In her mind, anything else was unthinkable.

"You know I love you," he whispered, and stroked her arm, "But you know you can't come with me now," he told her, "No matter how much I want you to."

She turned towards him and pulled him to her as she sobbed uncontrollably, with tears running down her cheeks. "Please," she sobbed, "Please take me with you …"

He tried to comfort her, holding her hard against his chest and stroking her neck with his free hand. "This is no life for you, Alice. You deserve better," he told her. Then he held her from him, and looked steadily into her eyes as he spoke. "When this season is over, I'll get a steady job. I'll find a flat somewhere, and get in touch with you. Then we can be together, and build a future together."

She lowered her eyes, then dried them with the back of her hand. "Do you promise?" she sobbed. "Do you really promise?"

"Of course I do," he told her. "You know I love you Alice. You know you're special." And he lowered his face to hers and kissed her again.

She came to the fairground early the next day. The funfair was gone, as though it had never been there at all. The music had been silenced. The blinking lights doused. All the stalls and amusements had been dismantled and were now packed on lorries and vans, ready to transport them to the next town.

She saw him standing in a group of people. He saw her and came towards her. They hugged and kissed. "Don't go," she begged. "Stay here."

He shook his head. "I've got to go, you know that."

Tears came to her eyes. "Will you come back to me?

He kissed her on the cheek. "You couldn't keep me away," he told her , and smiled into her sad face. "But we're done here for now, " he said. "The carnival is over. For now," he said. "But I'll be back, I promise."

The honking of a horn caught his attention and he turned his head. A driver was hanging out of a lorry door, waving for him to come.

He held her at arms length and looked into her eyes. "Got to go," he said.

They kissed. A final kiss, then he gently pulled himself from her embrace and ran to the lorry. He climbed on board, and waved to her as they drove away. He saw her reflection in the mirror, sobbing, her whole body shaking with sadness, her head bowed, miserable and forlorn, becoming smaller, fading away as the lorry accelerated, until it was finally gone.

The driver glanced at him and grinned. "A new town," he said, "and new possibilities," and gave a chuckle. The Big Wheel man sat in silence for a moment, thinking, then he turned to the driver and grinned back at him. "Yes," he said, "A new town and new possibilities," and they both laughed as the lorry accelerated towards the M1 that would take them to their next venue.

"Penny Lane is in my ears and in my eyes ..."
Penny Lane (Lennon & McCartney)
The Beatles 1967

Penny Lane

The Lollipop man balanced the stop-sign on his shoulder as he came down the street. The black cap on his head was slightly askew, as though to confirm that the uniform code was no longer valid. That he was now off duty, after once more having secured the safety of the school children as they crossed the main road, as they always did, twice a day.

He had worn the uniform and carried the stop sign for four years, since retirement, standing by the crossing and stopping the traffic to let the kids cross in safety. Twice a day, morning and afternoon. Although their exchanges were short, he felt that they got along well and that they liked him. Being local himself, he knew most of them by name, and most of their parents, so it was neither difficult to get along with them or to get their respect. After all, he was the Lollipop man, and he was there for them.

He heard the chiming of the ice-cream van as he opened the door to the house, and turned to see it coming around the corner and glide to a halt by the pavement. He called to his wife, "Do you want an ice-cream, Dot?" What he really meant, was "Can I have an ice-cream?" His wife had always looked after the housekeeping money, but it was a warm day, and it would be nice with an ice cream, so he repeated it, in case she had not heard him. "Do you want an ice-cream?" His wife found her purse and took out a few pennies. "I'll have a chock-bar," she told him as she handed him the money. "As though I didn't know," he laughed. She always wanted the chock-bar. But only when it was Wall's ice-cream, he acknowledged. For some reason she

167

would never have any other chock-bar. Only Wall's. If it wasn't Wall's, she would do without.

"Hello, Mr. Manning." A young girl passed by him on the pavement, holding a bottle of Lucozade in both hands. She came from the grocery store on the corner. "Is that for your mother?" he asked. She nodded her head. "Isn't she feeling better, yet?" She shook her head. "No, Mr. Manning," then moved down the street to number 37, and disappeared from the pavement through the door there.

There was a small queue at the van, and he joined it.

"Allright, Stan?" He was a small man, short and thin, with no teeth in his head and less hair on it. He wore a stained collarless shirt and crumpled trousers. The Lollipop man could remember when he had been younger, and better worn. Then, he had been a good footballer, an even better womanizer, and an infamous brawler who was often in trouble with both sexes. He had been a lively lad then, and quite handsome in his way, quick witted and fun to be with, and always popular with the women. But that had been long ago, when he still had his hair and his teeth. When he had become a widower, he seemed to lose all interest in his personal appearance, and obviously didn't care what people thought of him.

"Not so bad, thank you, Jim," he replied. They exchanged a few words as the queue began to disperse. The Lollipop man paid for his ice-creams and turned to go back to the house, only to be stopped by his neighbour, who drew him closer with a movement of the head indicating that he had something to tell him.

"You know Maggie Craddock around the corner?" he stated, rather than asked. Stan nodded his head, "Yes ..?" and wondered what was coming. "Died, last night, she did." He lifted his eyebrows and pouted his lips. "Happened like that!" and he snapped his fingers. "Poor old Donald," he said thoughtfully. "Must have been a hell of a shock." He had unwrapped his ice-cream and sucked at it through his toothless gums. "Anyway, see you in the pub tonight," he said, and stepped into the small living room of his house, leaving the door open behind him to let in air.

"Yes ... Poor old Donald," Stan thought. "And poor old Maggie." She hadn't been that old. In fact she was still quite young. He remembered her as

168

she had been, when the cheeful young nurse had moved into the street after she had married Donald. For some reason he could only picture her in her nurse's uniform, and still as the young woman she had once been. The fact that she had often worn the uniform when he had seen her, and that people always seemed to talk of "nurse Maggie" when they spoke of her, made the picture he now held in his mind seem quite natural. "God love us," he thought, "She couldn't have been more than forty!" He opened the door to the house. "Dot!" he called, ready to tell her the tragic news.

The bus stopped by the roundabout at the end of the Lane across the road from St. Barnabas. John Banks got off. The bus drove away, leaving him alone at the bus stop, unmoving, as he stared up Penny Lane, allowing the picture before him to print itself on his mind.

The thoughts that filled his head were too many to keep separate, but they filled him with memories that nourished the void that had been there for so many years. A smile played on his lips as he stood on the pavement with the traffic passing by on the street, and absorbed the atmosphere and the impressions around him. He noticed the distinct smell of the place, long forgotten, and his smile became broader. God, it was good to be back!

His parents had taken him to Australia when he was twelve. That had been ten years earlier. They had wanted a better future than the Liverpool of the 1950's could offer, and had emigrated to find it. He had found a new life Down Under, and a better one, but he had never forgotten Liverpool. He had never forgotten Penny Lane and the people who lived in its side streets. It had been his home, and, in spite of his new life in Australia, it always would be. Now he was finally back. Home.

He strolled slowly along the pavement, stopping often, to allow the memories to enfold him. Wanting them to. Bringing him back. Back to his childhood. Back to what had once been.

He stopped by the barber shop and looked through the window. He smiled happily. He was still there! The interior was the same as it always had been. Nothing had changed.

And there was Mr. Lamb with a customer in the chair, his harelip moving as he made conversation. It was as though the clock had been turned back ten years. Nothing had changed.

He remembered the question "Want your hair cut, son?" that he was always asked as he climbed into the chair, and how the harelip made the words lisp, and how all the kids used to mimic the barber behind his back and make fun of him. Now here he was ten years on, fondly watching the old man as he worked, and remembering him with pleasure.

Mr. Lamb had never been a good barber. Quite the contrary. But for some reason his customers stayed faithful to him, accepting the rather course treatment their hair received from his blunt scissors and the mindless conversation he invited them to be a part of. Back then, John Banks would have done anything to make his mother let him go to another barber, but now, looking at the old man through the window of the barber's shop, he was almost drawn to enter the establishment and climb into the chair once more.

"Want your hair cut, son?" He shook his head at the memory. It was always the same question whenever he got into the barber's chair. Always! Why else would he have been there? He had often been tempted to say, "No, I'm only here for the beer," or some such wise-crack, but he never did. Instead he would dutifully answer, "Yes, Mr. Lamb," and the shearing would begin.

He moved away from the window and continued down the pavement, looking closely at the people who passed by him, trying to recognise faces, but nobody seemed to notice him, and he saw none that he could remember. However, he did register that one or two seemed to give him a none-committal nod as they passed, and, when he looked around, he saw them glancing back at him with uncertainty on their faces, as though thinking, "Who was that?"

He passed by the grocer and looked inside, but saw nothing to attract his attention. How many times had he been sent there by his mother to buy various things she had forgotten on her own shopping trip? Yes, he thought, how many? He recalled his seventh birthday. His mother had told the grocer of the fact, and he had come from behind the counter with a scout's knife. "Here you are, son," he had said as he handed the knife to him. "You're old enough for this now." He had patted him on the head. "Happy birthday, son," he had said, and John Banks remembered it as though it had been yesterday.

He smiled at the memory, then chuckled as he recalled that he had cut his finger to the bone with the same knife later in the day. He remembered the blood and the howling of his mother as she covered it with a cloth and ran him to the doctor to be stitched. It had been an unpleasant experience at the time, but now it was just another fond memory that the sight of the grocery store had brought back to life.

As he crossed the road he noticed a familiar figure leaving the bank. It was the rolled umbrella that brought him back. It was a warm and sunny day, but the man carried an umbrella…? He looked closer and connected the features of the man before him with the memory of Mr. Jenkins the bank manager, and confirmed that it was the same man. A little older certainly, but still the same man. He remembered that he had never been referred to as Mr. Jenkins, but always as Mr. Jenkins, the bank manager. He smiled as he watched the man walk away, nodding his head to the people he passed.

The umbrella had been the give-away. He remembered his father joked about him and the fact that he never wore a coat no matter what the weather was like. He had claimed that it was because he wanted to show off what his father called "his banker's three-piece suit", wearing it like a uniform to confirm his stature in society. But he always carried an umbrella, regardless of the weather, holding it under his arm like the swagger stick of an army officer on parade. According to his father, Mr. Jenkins the bank manager, was always on parade.

The pub on the corner was just opening as he came to it, and the thought of having a beer crossed his mind, but he decided against it. It could wait. He was enjoying soaking up the atmosphere around him and watching the people as they passed, and he had been too young to know the inside of the local pub, which therefore held no memories for him. Perhaps later, he thought, and kept strolling, with his hands in his pockets and his eyes alive and searching.

The sound of a siren broke into his thoughts, and he stopped and watched as a fire engine drove down the road and soon disappeared from view, although the siren could still be heard for some time. He tried to recall the name. He had lived around the corner in a neighbouring street. It was a strange name. He tried to bring it back, and finally it came to him. Willingly! He remembered it now; William Willingly. But to the children of the area he was always Mr. Willingly, the fireman, and a man to be respected.

For some reason, none of the children in the area had made the obvious jokes about his name, although the potential was limitless. Instead they had held him in awe, having been told of his exploits as a fireman during the German bombing of the city in the war. The fact that he had supposedly been given some kind of award for bravery by the king himself had lifted him in their esteem, and, although he was an ordinary man in every way to look at, he had always seemed to them to be a big man, somehow larger than others.

He had noticed them once, as they had stood outside the open gates of the firestation looking in, and had fetched them inside and let them sit in the fire engine. He remembered the weight and size of the helmet he had good-naturedly placed on his head. "Now you're a fireman too, son," he had told him, with a smile on his face, and John Banks had felt pride filling him. But that had been many years ago, and Mr. Willingly the fireman, had probably retired long ago, he thought sadly, wishing it wasn't so.

As he passed two women, he overheard them talking. "…Yes … nurse Maggie! Can you believe it! And she wasn't even forty!"

He had long since forgotten her name, and could hardly remember her face, but it had all come back to him in a moment at the mention of her name. She had often been his babysitter when his parents had had to go out.

She had always been "Maggie" to him. From when he was still in nappies, until he was old enough to stay home alone. She had always been nice to him, and he still remembered her with affection although her face and her name had both passed into the shimmering oblivion of the past forgotten. But now, as though raised from the dead, it all came back to him.

The memory of the Queen's coronation day came back to him. Everybody had been out on the streets celebrating. There had been music and stalls and laughter all around. And uniforms of all kinds. They seemed to be everywhere; soldiers on leave, firemen, policemen, St. John's Ambulance people, scouts and guides. And nurses, like Maggie. She had taken him to a stall and let him help her to make tea and coffee that she served with sandwiches to anyone who had asked, and he had felt that by doing so he was in some strange way helping to celebrate the coronation. But most importantly, he felt some sense of pride at being with nurse Maggie in her uniform, and being allowed to help her. Now, he suddenly recalled her infectious laughter, hearing it in his mind as though she was there.

Nurse Maggie? That must be Maggie Craddock, he thought, and his curiosity forced him to ask them. "Excuse me," he said. "I couldn't help but hear you mention nurse Maggie. Do you mean Maggie Craddock?"

They considered him warily, while acknowledging the fact, "Yes …?" And who the hell are you? showed on their faces.

"Is something wrong?" he asked. "Has anything happened to her?"

The women looked after him as he walked away from them along the pavement, but now with a weight on his shoulder that had not been there before. Maggie, dead! It was a slap in the face, and a reminder that time did not stand still after all. That people had died since he had left. They had married, or divorced. Had children. Perhaps lost children. They had lived through good days and bad. Time had not stood still waiting for him to return to what had once been. Times had changed, and the people he had known had also changed. They had had their personal tragedies, and they had had good times, but he had not been a part of them, and he was therefore no longer a part of their lives, as he once had been, not having shared them for so long.

He felt like an imposter, imposing on their lives while pretending to be a part of them. For his own sake. Because a part of him felt the need to be a part of them. But now he realised that he no longer was. That this had only been a dream. Wishful thinking. Wanting to go back.

He suddenly felt lost and lonely, a stranger who did not belong there. He shouldn't have come back. It had all been an illusion. He should have lived with the memories.

Never go back! The reality will never equal the quality of the memories you carry with you, and disappointment will hit you in the stomach to make you retch and leave you feeling empty, while the memories you have nourished through the years with fondness and affection will be destroyed forever.

It was with such dark thoughts on his mind that he turned a corner and entered a side street coming off Penny Lane, and found himself looking down *his* street. The street where he had been born and raised.

Having been preoccupied by his thoughts, he had been unaware that he was entering his childhood's green and fertile valley, enclosed as it was, by two rows of grey and dirty brick houses pressing themselves against the pavement. The sudden sight of the familiar street with all its memories, shook the brooding from his mind, and he stood quite still, allowing his senses to come back to play as he surveyed the scene.

A few cars were parked against the pavement. A black Prefect, a Morris Minor and a three-wheeled Reliant. There had rarely been cars in the street when he had lived there. When one had stopped, the kids would all wander over to study it, and they would discuss the design and the speed it would do, as though they were connoiseurs. But most of all, they were interested in what it must have cost!

Three small boys were playing football, kicking the ball to each other, and he smiled again, seeing himself as a child once more, doing the same, and remembering the time the ball had gone through a neighbour's window. That had scared them! But looking at these children, it all now seemed so innocent, part of a distant past that only existed in his memory.

A couple of girls were playing with a toy pram, and for some reason reminded him of his first love. Helen White was sweet and ten. He was innocent and eleven, and in love. They had kissed once, short and sweet, and he had thought that he was quite a man, and that this meant that they were now going steady, and would eventually marry.

He laughed aloud, and quickly stemmed the sound as he heard it. Then chuckled quietly at the folly of the childish innocence he had once had.

He began to walk down the pavement, trying to remember the names and faces of the people who had lived there, and wondering if any of them still lived in the same houses they had inhabited when he had been a child and a part of their community.

A woman was leaning against the door post of her home, viewing the street with no particular interest as she smoked her cigarette. She turned towards him, idly eyeing him as he came closer, and he noticed that she lifted her head, as though suddenly aware of him.

"Hey!" she said, "Aren't you Johnny Banks?"

Before he could reply, she had moved inside the door, and he could hear her shouting, "Hey, Les, come and look! It's little Johnny from down the street!"

He smiled to himself. He was twenty-three, but still "little Johnny from down the street", and he suddenly felt a warm feeling creeping into him.

A man's face appeared from the opening in the door. He recognised it. "Hello, Mr. Dawson," he said to it.

"Bloody hell, Doris," the man said. "You're right! It is little Johnny". He came out on the pavement and looked at him. "It is, isn't it?" wanting it confirmed.

They shook hands. "What the bloody hell are you doing back here, son? How's your mum and dad? How are things going with you all down there? Is your dad with you? When …?"

His wife broke him off. "Lay off, Les! Give him a chance"

She noticed a woman coming down the street. "Lill!" she called out excitedly. "Look who's here. It's Johnny from down the street …"

He noticed that the children had stopped playing and were staring towards them with curiosity showing on their faces. The woman crossed towards them. A door had opened further down the street, and the faces of a man and a woman were almost comical as they strained out of the doorway to see what was happening. They reacted obediently to Doris's wave, "Come here," she called to them, "it's little Johnny!" and they too moved towards them along the pavement, forgetting to close the door behind them in their eagerness to be a part of the reunion.

There were smiles and questions, but Doris interrupted them all with her hands held high over him as though to protect him. "Don't frighten the poor boy," she said, "You'll scare him away, again." Then she turned to him and took him by the hand, and said, "Step inside, luv, and tell us everything!"

So they all went inside, and he told them.

It was good to be back!